MW01505661

Take Me To The Valley
Mountain Men of Whiskey River #8
Kaci Rose

Five Little Roses Publishing

Cover By: Wildheart Graphics

Edited & Proofed By: Debbe @ On The Page PA & Author Services

Contents

Mountain Men of Whiskey River

Take Me To The River – Axel and Emelie

Take Me To The Cabin – Phoenix and Jenna

Take Me To The Lake – Cash and Hope

Taken by The Mountain Man - Cole and Jana

Take Me To The Mountain – Bennett and Willow

Take Me To The Cliff – Jack and Sage

Take Me To The Edge – Storm and River

Take Me To The Valley – Evan and Calista

He's her brother's best friend. She's never had a thing for single dads or younger men... until him.

Evan

I've built my life around two things: protecting my daughter, Skye, and serving Whiskey River as a detective.

Love? It's off the table.

I can't have both—it's not fair to Skye, and I've already been burned once.

But when Calista Stapleton—the woman I've wanted for as long as I can remember—comes back to Whiskey River, all my carefully built walls start to crack.

She's my best friend's sister, and she's supposed to be off-limits.

But when I'm injured on the job and she steps in to take care of me and Skye, it feels like she's exactly where she's meant to be.

Calista

I've spent the last decade pouring myself into everyone else—patients, family, responsibilities.

Now I'm back home, hoping to reconnect with my family and start fresh.

But Evan Greer is here, too—my little brother's best friend, the man I've always tried to ignore.

He's strong, stubborn, and so fiercely protective of his daughter, it makes my heart ache.

When he gets hurt, and my brother insists I move in to help him recover, the fragile line we've been balancing on starts to disappear.

Every day with him and his daughter makes it harder to ignore the pull between us.

But he's my brother's best friend, and if this falls apart, it won't just be my heart on the line.

Do you like Military Men? Best friends brothers? What about sweet, sexy, and addicting books?

If you join Kaci Rose's Newsletter you get these books free!

https://www.kacirose.com/free-books/

Now on to the story!

Chapter 1

Evan

I remember the first time I held my daughter in my arms. Her mother was signing away her parental rights right there in the hospital room. I promised that little girl that I would fill her life with love, laughter, and friends. Since that day, it's been my sole purpose.

Standing in my new home outside the city limits in the Whiskey River Mountains, I think I finally made good on that promise. We have so many friends here today helping us move and unpack the house. More than I could have ever hoped for.

As soon as Axel's wife, Emelie, heard that I was moving, she enlisted all of their friends and their wives to help out. Who knew bringing a guy in for questioning on a possible kidnapping charge that turned out to be nothing would lead to a friendship like this?

I will never forget how protective Axel was of Emelie even then. I hope my daughter finds a man like him one day.

The mountain men of Whiskey River Montana are super protective of each other. They have slowly welcomed me into their circle, and now that I have moved to the mountains, that protection includes both my daughter and me.

"Daddy! Daddy! Daddy!" my daughter, Skye, comes running down the stairs, laughing and calling for me.

In that moment when I turn to watch her with a huge smile on her face and her dark brown hair flowing behind her with curls at the end of it, she looks so much like her mother.

"Yes, princess?" I ask, bending down to scoop her up.

"Jenna said Willow is going to help her decorate my room as a princess room, but I had to ask you first. So, can we? Please, please, please?" She asks in a high-pitched, excited voice while she giggles at me.

She makes it impossible to say no, not that I ever would. I knew when we moved in, she would want to decorate her room. Granted, I kind of hoped she would want a camp or nature room over a pink princess room, but if that is what she wants, then that is what she gets.

"Of course you can." I set her down and pull out my phone. "Just in case that's what you decided, I ordered you this princess bed canopy. It will be here next week."

"Daddy!" Skye screeches, giving me a huge hug. It's like the one she has been hinting at, but according to Sage, Jack's wife, who I ordered it through when I was in town last, it's better because it has fairy lights in it. Apparently, that's a big deal with things like this.

Looks like she was right, and I owe her one when I see her next.

"Go make plans with the girls so they can tell me what you need, and I can get it ordered," I say as she bounces off.

She has so much energy. Just like her mom does, it's what attracted me to her and made me think it was love. I wanted it to be love, but when she got pregnant and told me she was putting the baby up for adoption, the illusion shattered.

It's for the best. I got my little princess and realized I wanted to be in love with someone so badly I had even tricked myself. After that, I swore off dating because I couldn't risk masking my true feelings again and hurting my Skye.

"This place needs some work, but I think it's perfect for you," Cody says, walking up beside me.

He and I have been best friends since we were in diapers. His family owns the whiskey distillery in town that recently opened up.

"I think so too. Plus, I need to find some busy work this winter," I agree.

"You still thinking of retiring from the force?" He asks in a lower tone because he knows he's the only one I've told. It's a small town, and the last thing I need is for that to get out and around town before I have even talked to my boss.

"Yeah, I like the idea, but what would I do? Plus, I don't think it's the right time after I just moved in. Before I make a bigger decision like that, I need to settle in."

"I agree. Next week, sometime after one o'clock, we should grab a drink and make one of those pro-con lists you love so much and see where you end up," he jokes.

I know he thinks it's all good fun. But the pro-con lists have helped me make some of the best choices in my life. When I skipped the list, I made some of the worst. Though it doesn't stop him from poking fun at me about them any chance he gets.

"Alright, just let me know for sure. By mid-week, Skye will be ready for your mom's home-cooked meal. Since we will be living on frozen meals until the new kitchen appliances get here."

They were among a few more things I had ordered from Sage and Jack. Because of how remote we are, it will take longer than I planned for them to be shipped here. Once they arrive, I will have the guys help me get them to the cabin.

It takes more work, but it's the tradeoff for living in the mountains. One thing I'm excited about is to finally be living out of town. Skye is enthusiastic, too, but I don't know if it's because I'm excited or if it's because she truly is. Either way, I plan to make sure she loves it out here as much as I do.

Though I didn't move as far into the mountains as Bennett and Cole have. This way, I can still easily get to town in the winter. I have to with my job and Skye's school. But it's enough that I have some mountain views and land and can be much more self-sustainable.

"Well, I'll let you know for sure when we can meet," Cody says, interrupting my thoughts. "Mom will make that mac and cheese Skye loves. Bring her after school, and they can make it together."

"I think she'd love that," I say as I watch Axel pull Emelie into a hug and kiss the top of her head.

While I won't ever admit it out loud, I want that. I want a mom for Skye, and I want to come home to this house and to my sweetheart and build a life together. Who knows, maybe it can still happen, but right now, I have to build my life as it is.

"Oh, I meant to tell you. I saw Skye's mom on a commercial the other day for some insomnia drug. She's hitting the big time now, huh?" Cody laughs.

Skye's mother signed over her rights, got clearance from her doctor and went to Hollywood so fast it made my head spin. She's had a few small parts on some soap shows, and now she's in this commercial. Seven years in and she still hasn't had that big break. Nothing worth showing Skye, anyway.

We haven't heard from her, and I prefer it that way. Skye doesn't ask about her much, but I try to keep it positive. She knows her mom is an actress in Hollywood and just couldn't be a mommy. Hopefully, she understood.

Though I know someday, she will have more questions, and I dread that day. Thankfully, that isn't today.

"Keep that to yourself. Skye isn't asking questions about her mom, and I'd like to keep it that way as long as possible."

"She will someday, though," he says.

"Then I'll pull up her Wikipedia page and explain it all."

"What are you two gossiping about?" Storm asks.

"Someone we knew growing up. Nothing important," Cody covers for me.

He might give me shit, but he has my back at every turn, and for that I'm grateful.

"Thank fuck!!" Storm says. "I'm just far enough away from where I grew up to not run into anyone I know unless I want to. Now, I'm taking off to get home to my wife and son. Let me know when the appliances get here and I'll come help you get them up the mountain and installed."

I nod, and he says goodbye to everyone else and heads out. Not long after, everyone else begins to leave, and before I know it, it's just me and Skye. Her eyes are starting to droop as she sits on the couch, leaning on me.

"Okay, Princess. It's time to get ready for bed. It's been a long day, and there is more unpacking to do tomorrow," I say. Then I scoop her up in my arms as dramatically as I can and toss her over my shoulder, which causes her to giggle.

We run through her bedtime routine, and once she is in bed, it's obvious something is on her mind.

"What is going through that head of yours?" I ask.

"Will you sleep with me, Daddy, just tonight?"

I know it's a new house with new sounds and shadows. No wonder she's a little nervous and scared.

"How about I lie with you until you fall asleep? If you wake up and are scared, you can get in bed with me."

She nods, handing me the princess book she has me reading to her each night. Before I'm even halfway, Skye is fast asleep. Soaking in the moment, I watch my child sleep so peacefully, and I stay a little longer.

I let the enjoyment of the first night in our new home and the start of life I want for her and for myself seep into me.

It's understandable why Skye is scared. I am, too, in a different way, though it's the fear that comes with excitement to start a new journey.

I can't wait to see what the future brings.

Though I just wish it had given me some warning.

Chapter 2
Calista

I'm less than an hour from my childhood home and almost twelve hours into my trip today, and I'm starting to question everything.

When my brother called and found out I was between jobs, it should have been a warning sign, but I didn't listen. He convinced me to come home and help with the distillery that my four brothers started because it was doing so well.

It wasn't until after I agreed and had my moving truck loaded, and was on the way to Whiskey River, did they mention they needed help with Dad, too. His health was declining faster than Mom let on, and she can't do it all herself.

Being a nurse and between jobs right now, they thought I'd be the perfect one to help out. Even though their logic is sound, it's not something I want to do. I had made them swear they wouldn't dump it all on me, and now they're trying to once again. Before I know it, they'll be depending on me too much because I'm home and it's convenient for them. It's one of the many reasons I left. I needed my own life.

As I round a corner, a deer darts across the road. I miss it by just a few inches, making my heart race. Maybe crossing the Whiskey River Mountains for the first time in years at night wasn't such a great idea. But now I'm just determined to get into town and relax.

My family doesn't think I'm getting in until tomorrow, so I can head right to my rental and have a day of peace before they descend on me. That's why I decided to drive straight through instead of stopping for the night.

I love my family, but with four brothers, it can be a bit much. They are super protective. Even though I'm older than three of them, they still treat me like I'm a baby and need to be taken care of. I hated it in school. If someone so much as said one bad word about me, the four of them were jumping or picking a fight with that person. Now, as an adult, I appreciate it, but I still need my space.

It also doesn't hurt that my best friend in the whole world still lives in Whiskey River. Kaylee and I both left to go to school and then she moved back to Whiskey River while I moved away. We still talk multiple times a day, and we visited each other or took friend-cations multiple times a year, but it will be really nice to be closer.

The day I told her I was moving back to Whiskey River, Montana, she let out a squeal that was so loud that I'm sure they heard her down in Utah.

As I round one of the sharper curves on the mountain, the sight that greets me has me slamming on my breaks. There is a car that has run off the side of the road. The guardrail seems to have stopped it, but the tail end of the car is pointing up in the air, all the lights are still on, and the tires are spinning like the incident just happened.

Pulling my car off to the side of the road, I turn on the flashers and grab my phone as I run over to the other car. There is a woman in the car, unconscious, with blood on her forehead and face. She is alone in the car, and it looks like a tree has stopped her from going over the edge. Since everything seems to be stable, I check my phone and I'm grateful to find I have service.

"911, what's your emergency?" a woman answers my call.

"I'm on Whiskey Mountain and came up on a car that crashed over a guardrail and into a tree. A young woman in the car is unconscious and bleeding from her head," I tell her.

After asking me a few questions about the location, she asked me to stay on the phone with her.

"She is starting to come to. I'm an RN with some emergency experience," I say.

"What is going on? Where am I?" The woman in the car asks.

"Hi, I'm Calista, please don't move. You've been in a car crash. Help is on the way," I tell her.

Her hand goes to her head, and she moans when she sees the blood.

"There was a bear.... On the road," she groans.

"Ma'am, a deputy is a few minutes out. EMS is still ten minutes out," the 911 operator says.

Then she has me run through a list of questions to ask the woman in the car.

I find out she was heading home to Helena after spending the day in Whiskey River. While her memory seems to be intact, she's hazy and is fading in and out. Patiently, I ask the rest of the questions: can she move her arms and legs, is she in pain, and did she hit her head?

We finish the questions just as flashing blue lights and sirens fill the air. Relief hits me that someone is here to help her, but I know my night is far from over. There will be a million questions. I sigh, letting go of my fantasies of a lazy, quiet night before everyone invades my new apartment.

"The officer is here," I tell the dispatcher, and we end the conversation.

I put the phone in my pocket as the officer walks up. When I look up, our eyes meet and he freezes on his way to the car. I smile at those familiar hazel green eyes. "Evan Greer?" I ask. I'm shocked that of all the people in town, he is who I run into when I'm trying to sneak in undercover.

Even though I know my brothers will know I'm in town before I even get to my doorstep, I can't help but smile. Evan is my younger brother's best friend and one of my favorites of my brothers' friends.

"Calista?" Evan asks, shock clear in his voice.

Then, shaking his head, he moves to the front of the crashed car. I lean against the guardrail, making sure I stay out of the way while he talks to the woman in the car.

Once the ambulance shows up, they take over, and Evan comes walking over to me. It's hard for me to combine the rail-thin, crazy as my brother, full of energy kid he was in high school with the man that fills out a police uniform like no one should, who is standing in front of me.

"Your brother said you weren't getting in until tomorrow," he says at my side as we both watch the EMTs do their job.

"I was trying to sneak in under the radar to have a peaceful night to myself before they swarmed my place tomorrow. So much for that," I sigh.

"Well, I won't say anything until I see Cody again, which won't be for a few days," he says.

"That would be amazing. I love my family, but…" I trail off, not sure I want anything I say to get back to them.

"But you've gotten used to being on your own, and they are a bit much?" He fills in.

"Yeah," I agree.

"I get it. They have me over for dinner regularly, and even still, after all these years, it's overwhelming. I don't know if I'll ever get used to it," he says, smiling.

For a moment there, I forgot to breathe. What the hell? This is Evan. Not only is he my brother's best friend, he is six years younger than me. It's probably my body just reacting to the fact that I haven't been laid nor had a serious relationship in over a year. I'm going to have to have a date with a toy packed in my car that will take care of that issue.

"Cody said you joined the department. I'm kind of shocked to see you working nights, though," I say, thinking he should have been promoted to day shift by now. He's been there long enough.

"Normally, I do. But the guy who had the shift tonight is a friend of mine, and he had a family thing. Skye is with your parents tonight, so I took the shift to help him out."

"Skye?" I ask, feeling a pool of jealousy in my gut that I hate is even there. I know my family would have mentioned if he was getting married, so I can only assume it's a long-term girlfriend. Though I'm shocked at how much I hate the thought of him with anyone. I have to remind myself he isn't mine, nor could he ever be, and I want him happy, at least for my brother's sake.

"My daughter," he says with a smile lighting up his face.

"Oh, that's right. How old is she now?" I ask, trying not to let the relief show on my face.

"She will be seven soon. With your mom's help, she is planning a big, elaborate party. I know there is going to be a lot of pink and glitter," he laughs.

Even though I knew he had a daughter, I was so wrapped up in my life that I had never thought much about it. I guess I never realized he had her so young. Everything in me wants to ask about her mother, but that isn't my place, so I refrain.

"I can't say I ever pictured you as a girl dad," I laugh.

"Well, that makes two of us. Let me go check with the EMTs. Then I just have a few basic questions, and you can get on with your sneaking into town," he says, winking at me. Then as he goes over to check on the EMTs who just got the woman onto a stretcher, I enjoy watching him walk.

He is definitely a flirt. I bet he has all the women in town falling at his feet, just like my brothers do.

As the EMTs load the woman into the ambulance, a tow truck pulls up, parks on the shoulder in front of my car, and waits for the ambulance to get out of the way.

Evan walks back over to me with a notepad and pen in hand.

Once again, I go over the entire story of finding the car, what I saw when I walked up, calling 911, and all the details. He asks a few questions, like if I saw any cars or animals in the area before or after I stopped, and I tell him I hadn't. Before we finish up, I give him all my information for the report.

"Well, you are free to go. But," he pauses, reaching into his pocket, and pulls out a card. Then, flipping it over, he scribbles something on the back. "Text me when you get home so I know you made it. Your brother will never forgive me if I don't make sure you make it safely."

Taking the card from him, I put it in my pocket. "Will do. Thank you for not ratting me out to them."

"Hey, you saved my ass a few times growing up. It's about time I get to repay the favor." He smiles again, tipping his hat at me before walking back to his police car.

I head to my car, taking a few deep breaths. Why was the way he walks and talks, and let's face it, his muscular body so damn sexy? Damn it, get it together. This is Evan, not some stranger you just met.

Carefully, I make my way down the mountain and to the apartment I rented above one of the stores downtown. It's temporary until I find a place. At least this one is furnished, so only minimal unpacking is needed.

I follow the check-in instructions and once inside, lock the door behind me.

Then, exhausted, I flop down on the couch. Well, I made it into town, and as long as Evan keeps his word, I will have a morning of peace. Taking the card out of my pocket, I enter the cell phone number Evan scribbled on the back. I save it on my phone and text him.

> **Me:** I made it home. Thank you for everything.

> **Evan:** It was really good to see you. Save my number, and let me know if you need anything.

> **Me:** Saved. See you around.

> **Evan:** You can count on it.

Chapter 3

Evan

O f all the people to run into last night, Calista Stapleton was at the bottom of the list of people I'd have guessed. Hell, let's be honest, she wasn't even on the list. Why hadn't Cody mentioned she was moving home sooner when he helped me move into my cabin last weekend?

In all fairness, that was the first time we had been able to sit down together in almost a month. Will she be at the family dinner this weekend? I'm sure she will. There is no way Calista will get out of it since it's the first time she's been home in ages.

"The hospital is calling with an update on the woman from the crash last night," Judy, the sheriff's office receptionist, says. She has been here longer than I have. She is in her late forties and does whatever is needed around the office from answering calls, being anyone's secretary, and even keeping us all organized. Right after I started here, Judy was the one who took on the task of fully digitizing the office.

"Thank you," I say, but she hesitates by my desk, so I know she has a non-work-related question. Judy is also one of the town's gossips.

"What is it?" I ask.

"How did she look?" She asks with slightly more excitement than I think the situation warrants.

"She had blood on her forehead and was confused," I say, making Judy frown. "I'll let you know more once you let me pick up this phone."

"Evan! I meant Calista. I can't believe the family kept her coming back to town a secret! We would have thrown her a welcome home party!" Judy sighs.

"That might be why they kept it a secret so they could spend some time with her."

Picking up the phone, I talk to the nurse at the hospital over in Helena. Apparently, the woman insisted that she be taken there.

The woman, Becca, who isn't a local, was just visiting and didn't know the mountain. She swears she swerved because there was a bear on the road, but there was no sign of a bear in the area. That doesn't mean there wasn't one, but it also means it could have been a shadow. That's between her and her insurance company.

Judy stays by my desk listening to my side of the conversation, which is mostly my grunting my way through the nurse, talking a mile a minute and telling me about the patient. Later today, she will be released to the care of her husband since she has a mild concussion and needed a few stitches on her forehead. She also has a sprained ankle and broken arm, but otherwise was very lucky.

Once off the phone, I relay that information to Judy, and she runs off back to her desk to call her friends and spread the news, I'm sure. I pull up the report on the accident and fill in the details from my call and get ready to close it out when I see Calista's name. I pause.

When she left for college, I had the biggest crush on her. I would count down the days, looking forward to when she'd come home for a visit. I was too young for her to pay any attention to me back then. After she graduated, she moved away, and I haven't seen her since. Her family has gone out to visit her, but she really hasn't been back to Whiskey River. I thought I might be over that little schoolboy crush, but I'm thinking maybe not. Because the feeling I've had for her since last night is even stronger than I remember all those years ago.

I glance at my notepad, where I wrote her phone number from the report and before I even left the scene, she had added her number to my phone. I'm sure she'd like an update, to let her know the woman is all right. After checking my email, there is still nothing on the drug case I've been working on, so I grab my phone and think about calling her. At the last moment, I decide not to call. I don't know what her plans are now that she's back or if she is working. So I send her a text,

> **Me:** Hey, it's Evan. I just talked to the hospital and thought you'd want to know the woman from last night is doing well and will make a full recovery.

> **Calista:** That's great! I really appreciate you letting me know. Everyone has been asking because the story has already made its way around town.

> **Me:** I told you I could keep it quiet last night, but as soon as people started reading my report on the accident, it would be all over Whiskey River.

> **Calista:** Small town grapevine 101. I kind of missed it, but just didn't miss being part of it. I will let you get back to work. Thank you for the update.

Me: Call anytime.

Calista: Thanks again.

I check my email and there's still nothing. I've been working on this drug case, and I'm waiting for some intel to come in from the guy watching the house right now. If he has nothing to report, that means all is quiet, which is good in that no drugs are passing hands, but bad because it slows the case down. The sooner we can close out this case, the sooner we can get the drugs off the streets of Whiskey River.

Since there is still nothing new for me, I give Cody a call.

"Hey man, what's up?" he answers. I can hear the noise from the distillery behind him. "You got a minute to talk?" I ask, knowing how crazy that place can get.

"Yeah, Colton is here, and he can hold it down for a bit," he says as the noise muffles in the background, so I assume he stepped into his office and closed the door.

"Yeah, until some skirt walks in," I laugh.

Colt is a town playboy and has had that reputation since high school. He's happy, responsible, and upfront with the ladies, so it works for him. If it's what he enjoys, more power to him. Even if his mom drops hints about settling down, his family has been supportive. But he's the baby of the family, and since his older brothers haven't settled, he has no intentions either. Colt has invested a chunk of money in the distillery, and he knows better than to let some girls get in the way of the business.

"What's up?" Cody asks.

"Why didn't you tell me Calista was moving back to town sooner?" I ask him outright.

We have been friends for so long that there is no beating around the bush when we have something to say. That is one of the best parts of our friendship.

Cody pauses and doesn't answer right away, but I know he heard me.

"How did you find out?" he asks.

"I forget you seem to be immune to town gossip. Last night there was an accident on Whiskey Mountain, a car off the side of the road. Calista was the one who called it in and was there when I got on the scene. Yes, she is fine," I say because I know it's his next question.

"Calista asked us to keep it quiet and we haven't had a chance to talk before you moved," Cody says. "With everyone there it didn't seem the right time to bring it up. She was hoping to have some space before the town found out. You know she hates being the center of attention."

"A text works too, you know," I say, but I understand why he didn't tell me, and I'm not mad about it either.

"Come down for a drink any time, and we can talk 'til your little gossip heart is content," he ribs at me.

"Fuck you," I laugh.

"Is the person who was in the crash okay?" He asks, his tone more serious.

"Yes. I just heard from the hospital that she will make a full recovery. Just banged up," I say.

"Anyone we know?"

"Nope. Someone who was in town for the day and shouldn't have been driving the mountain at night. She was lucky your sister found her, or she could have sat there for a few hours before another car passed," I say.

"I'm going to have a talk with Calista about driving that mountain at night."

"Cody, she is older than you and was the one who taught you to drive that mountain," I laugh.

"Well, still sneaking into town in the middle of the night? What was she thinking?"

"That she wanted a quiet night to settle in before you guys ascended on her," I supply.

"You are sticking up for her now?"

"Just relaying what she said. How many times do you need a break from family? You guys are close, but sometimes it can also be a bit much."

Growing up, I loved his big family because I wished I had brothers who were close like he does. My younger sister and I never really got along because of the large age gap between us. Once she graduated high school, she moved to Florida to work on cruise ships. Her visits home are infrequent, and it's been a while.

But at the same time, even though I wished to be part of Cody's family, they were overwhelming and a lot too. But I'm thankful they will be there for Skye and give her the grandparents she won't have now that my parents have passed.

"Don't have to tell me that. How many times have I enlisted you to help me hide from them growing up?"

"I think our makeshift tree fort is still there if you need a break," I joke.

"Get back to writing jay walking tickets. Some of us have real work to do. See you at dinner this weekend," he says.

Sitting there for a minute after I hang up with Cody, I wonder how I'm going to navigate their family dinners with my daughter and the weird feelings I have for his sister.

"Check your email," Judy singsongs as she walks past my desk.

Shaking my head, I pull up my email, finally seeing a report from my guy. There's been movement on the place we are watching. We have enough to bust this guy who is selling, but we are trying to hold off to find out who his supplier is and try to take them down, too.

It would be great to get them both, but we can't hold out forever.

Chapter 4
Calista

Today, I'm biting the bullet and heading to my parents' house to visit my dad. The true reason I was asked to come home was because of his declining health and Mom needing help to take care of him.

The distillery my brothers started in town is taking off, and they swear they need help there. But the reality is my parents are getting older and need help, so my brothers want me here to help with Mom and Dad, so they don't have to   .

Every time I would talk to Mom on the phone, she'd swear up and down they were fine, and she was able to keep up. But then I'd get a different story from my brothers. So, I figure before I make too many plans, I should see my parents with my own eyes. After my brothers go to the distillery for the day, I'm having brunch with them so there is no chance of the guys popping in. I don't want them trying to influence my opinion of how our parents are doing.

As a nurse, one thing I learned is to assess a patient one-on-one because the parents or the child will make things worse than they are or feed you a different narrative. After that, I talk to the caretakers, and sometimes they have more info, but most of the time, they are worried about something small.

When I pull into my childhood home, I find my dad sitting on the front porch swing with his dog, Wolfgang, lying with his head in my dad's lap. Wolfgang is a scary-looking German Shepard with a heart of gold. But don't let it fool you; he's protective too. A person working on the power line found out the hard way when they walked into the yard where they weren't supposed to be.

When I pull in, Wolfgang jumps up and barks until I step out of the car. He knows me from all the times my parents brought him to visit, so as soon as he realizes who it is, he runs down the porch to greet me, covering me in slobber.

"Hey, sweet pea. Looks like he's as happy for you to be here as I am." Dad stands to greet me as I walk up on the porch.

Though he's a little slow to get up, he's steady on his feet once he's up. Dad wraps me in a tight hug as Wolfgang pushes between us to get in on the action.

"Missed you. So glad you're home," Dad says as he holds me tight.

"Missed you too," I whisper, fighting back tears at the sound of the emotion in my dad's voice.

"Well, let's head inside and let your mom fawn all over you," Dad says as we pull away. Before going inside, we both pet Wolfgang and give him the attention he thinks he deserves.

"She's here!" Dad calls out, and the noise in the kitchen stops. My mom comes running down the hallway in her 1950s-style dress with her apron swooshing around her. She was the original pin-up girl before it was really a thing.

"Oh, you're here!" She pulls me into a hug. "Your brothers said you looked good, but you know how they are," she waves her hand and goes back to the kitchen.

The other day, my brothers came and helped me unpack and move into the apartment. They insisted that Mom and Dad stay home. We all agreed we didn't want them going up and down the stairs since they're steep. I like that my place is directly above one of the shops.

My brothers are already trying to convince me to move in with the parents instead of staying in town. Hence my visit today before I make my choice.

"Come, keep me company. The food will be done shortly," Mom calls to me.

Dad and I follow her to the back of the house, where the kitchen opens to a large dining room. Beyond that, we have a spacious great room that easily fits all of us. The fireplace is going, and the dining room table is already set for three. Dad and I sit at the kitchen island because Mom doesn't want us in her way. But she wants us near so she can talk.

"Now, I'm not happy you snuck into town in the dead of night, but I'm glad you were there to help that poor woman!" Mom says as she stirs the gravy on the stove.

"Evan called and told me she is doing fine. She was very lucky," I say.

My parents exchange a look that I can't read before my mom continues.

"Why did Evan call you?" she asks casually.

"Because I asked him to update me when he knew. I was worried, and she was really out of it when they loaded her into the ambulance. How did you find out about all this?"

"Small town, sweetheart. Evan called Cody, but I also heard it from Judy, who also called to make sure you were okay too," Mom says.

"Even Jack heard about it and called to check in," Dad says.

Jack owns the outdoor store, which also serves as the hub where everyone goes for information, as well as to order items they can't get in town. The families that live in the mountains rely heavily on him. In addition, he also sells many handmade items there that townspeople make.

He gets a lot of his business from tourists on their way from Yellowstone National Park to Glacier National Park or vice versa since we are a good stop between the two.

Once my mom serves breakfast at the table, we talk and catch up before my dad and I take over cleaning. Dad always said if my mom cooks, she isn't cleaning the kitchen too. Once the kitchen is clean, we join Mom on the couch by the fire.

"You know, your sons made it seem like you two were on death's door and wouldn't survive without me moving in to help," I say sarcastically.

They both start laughing.

"I had a feeling they would go that route. We were all talking about how much we missed you. Once we found out you were between jobs they started their scheming to get you home," Dad says.

"We won't be running in the Boston marathon anytime soon, but we are doing fine. Your room is ready for you whenever you want it," Mom says.

"I think I want to get my own place in town. I have the apartment until spring, so I have time to look for my own space."

Fortunately, I was able to rent the apartment in the off-season. Normally it is a short-term rental for people passing through. My best friend, Kaylee, helped me find the place. She says it normally sits empty in the winter, so the landlord was happy to have the income.

"I figured you would," Dad chuckles.

"But if you ever need it, I'm willing to move in and take care of you two," I say.

"We will keep that in mind," Mom says.

"So, will you be helping your brothers at the distillery?" Dad asks.

"They said they needed help, but I don't know if that was another lie to get me here or not," I say.

"Oh, they need help, Mom says. "That place has exploded since they opened. They have expansion plans already in the works."

"You should go down and check it out when you leave here," Dad urges me.

I nod but don't commit to anything.

"I might look and see if the doctor's office is hiring even if I just work part-time. I need to work to transfer my license and keep it active," I say.

"That's a good idea. Dr Hamilton retired, but the new doctor is really nice. She is looking for help too, last I heard," Mom says.

Interesting. I love working for female doctors, but even more, I want to know she took over the practice from Dr Hamilton because he had no desire to retire. Well, that was the last gossip I heard, anyway.

After talking some more, I say my goodbyes and am given strict orders to not be late for dinner this weekend. I promise and then get back in my car.

Mom and Dad are doing well. The house is clean and maintained, but they have definitely declined since I saw them at Christmas. Dad isn't as steady on his feet, and Mom looks thinner and pale. I think I can help take some of the burden off of them. Even if I was manipulated to be here, I'm glad to be home.

I drive by the distillery, but I don't stop. Mom will no doubt have given them a heads-up, but I want to completely surprise my brothers when I stop in. Besides, I need to hit the grocery store and stock up for a few days. Though I think I'm going to go home after this and work on unpacking the last of the boxes and get settled in.

Driving by the distillery, I can't help but feel proud of my brothers. They have been talking about building this place for a while. They have been planning and dreaming of it, and here it is. It's pretty busy for a Tuesday afternoon off-season, and the parking lot is decently full. There are people filling the patio under the warmers, taking in the beautiful mountain view. I see Cody talking to a group of people by the door, and there are lots of smiles on happy faces.

Glad I decided to drive by, I head toward my apartment downtown. Once inside, I open the curtain in the living room window and enjoy the mountain vista and natural light. Then I go into the kitchen and unpack my new coffee maker that I picked up this morning. I am not a morning person, so coffee is a must, and the tiny one cup at a time coffee maker would not cut it on a day-to-day basis with me.

I'm setting it up on the counter when my phone rings. The screen says it's from Evan. Why would he be calling? Maybe he has another update on the woman from the other night, so I pick it up.

"Hello?" I ask as more of a question.

"Calista," he says, and I can hear the smile in his voice.

"Everything okay?" I ask because I can't think of another reason he'd be calling me.

"Yeah, I talked with your dad, and he said you had brunch there today. I wanted to see how much your brothers' story matches up," he laughs.

"Not at all."

"I figured. I also wanted to see how you were settling in and if you needed any help moving in or unpacking."

"I'm okay for now. My brothers helped with the big stuff already. But I'm going to be looking for something more permanent. When I move all my stuff from storage, I will one hundred percent take you up on it. You will live to regret that offer."

"I doubt it, but I'm happy to help if you need it. I'm sure I can rope a few guys from the station to come help, too."

"Between you and my brothers, you will have the whole damn town helping." I sigh, wishing I was over-exaggerating that claim, but I'm not.

"Hang on," he says, and then there is some muffled whispering on his end, but I can't make out any of it. He must have his hand over the phone.

"Judy says to tell you the doctor's office is hiring part-time," he says, and then there is more whisper-ing. "She already told them you'd be coming by."

"Tell Judy I said hi and thank you. You know I only mentioned that to my parents less than two hours ago. I think the gossip vine around here has gotten faster over the years," I chuckle.

"The faster the internet, the faster the gossip," he says, making us both laugh.

Since we haven't really talked in ages, we take some time to catch up. He asks about my life away from home and I find out about his career on the force. Before I know it, an hour has gone by, and I've set up the coffee machine.

"Have we really been talking for an hour?" I ask, shocked.

"Looks like it. I better go pick up Skye. See you this weekend," he says.

I'm looking forward to this family dinner more than any other one before it. Maybe I know why, but I'm not admitting it.

Chapter 5
Evan

As I pull into Cody's parents' place, I park my car and take a few minutes, like I do every day, to leave work at work and refocus on being present with my daughter. Dealing with this drug case is taking a toll on me, but I have never brought my work home before, and I don't plan to start now. Thankfully, Maggie and Don understand and will keep her occupied until I walk through the door. They are heaven-sent. Not only do they watch her for me after school, but they help her with homework. For now, at her age, it's mostly reading and spelling words.

Once I feel like I've fully left work at the office, I step out of my car and go inside. I don't knock. When I was a kid and knocked, I'd get in trouble because Maggie would tell me I was family, and family doesn't make her get up from the couch to open the door for them.

"It smells like cookies!" I call out, opening the front door to the delicious smell of Maggie's chocolate chip cookies filling the air.

"Daddy!" Skye squeals and comes running to me from the kitchen. "We made cookies for a snack, and I got to mix and lick the spoon!"

It's pretty obvious because there is flour on her shirt and chocolate smeared on her face.

"She didn't have homework today and got a one hundred on her spelling test, so I thought we'd celebrate." Maggie greets me with a kiss on my cheek as I walk into the kitchen.

When I set the lunch box Maggie insists on packing me on the counter, she takes it and packs leftovers from whatever they had for dinner last night in it. I then put it in the fridge so later I can take it home and have it for lunch at work. She claims to prepare it for me because she can't cook for just two and feels bad about it going to waste. I think it's her way of taking care of me, and I let her do it because Maggie is the best cook I know.

"That's amazing, princess! Way to go on your spelling test! We have to stop at the grocery store on the way home. How about you pick out what you want for dessert tonight?" I set her on the kitchen counter and grab a paper towel to clean her up.

"Anything?" She asks, excitement in her voice.

I pause because I know a setup when I hear one. But she's seven, so how bad can it be?

"Within reason," I say to cover my bases.

"I want one of those unicorn ice cream sundaes Nana and I saw on the TV yesterday," she says.

The happy excitement on her face is something I'd do almost anything to see, but I have no idea what she is talking about, so I look over at Maggie, who is on her phone.

"Unicorn Sundae? Do they sell them at the Whiskey River grocery store?" I ask.

"You have to make it, silly," Maggie says, showing me a video on her phone.

The unicorn sundae is more sugar than Skye gets in a year combined. It's a chocolate-coated waffle bowl, not a cone, but a bowl that holds six scoops of blue, pink, and purple ice cream. The ice cream is topped with bright blue frosting and glitter sprinkles. Then, if that's not enough sugar, a large lollypop is stuck in. They've added candy eyes and corn to make it look like a unicorn.

"Good lord, who even eats that?" I hand back Maggie's phone.

"Please, Daddy?" Skye begs.

"Let's see what the store has, and we can make a much smaller version with one scoop of ice cream," I say, attempting to compromise.

"See, I knew you wouldn't say no!" Skye jumps off the counter and runs to get her backpack and I know I've been played.

"She asked me yesterday, and I said you would tell her no. Heck, I would have said no," Maggie laughs and starts putting the cookies away.

Once Skye has all her things and goodbyes are said, Maggie reminds me once again that tomorrow is picture day and to make sure Skye dresses up. Finally, we are out the door.

On the way to the store, she tells me all about her day. She says she had pizza for lunch and that we should have spaghetti for dinner so she can keep the Italian theme going. She tells me how her friend Becky's family has plans to go camping in Yellowstone and when we can go. Then she asks twenty questions about Yellowstone and makes me promise to take her this summer.

Every summer, we go on a small trip—just her and me. Last year, it was to Bozeman, Montana, because she was obsessed with dinosaurs. We visited the museum there and part of the dinosaur trail. However, I don't start planning anything until a few months ahead of time because she changes her mind at the drop of a hat.

We go inside the store and grab a cart. She likes to push the cart, and I steer to make sure she doesn't crash into anyone. I pull up the list on my phone that I had made over the last few days with dinners to get us through the weekend. When we get to the baking aisle, we look for items to make her mini version of a unicorn sundae.

"Look Daddy! Glitter sprinkles! They have them!" Skye jumps and points to them on the shelf.

"You know, I think I'd have reacted the same way if they had glitter sprinkles when I was a kid," a familiar voice says behind me.

I turn to find Calista with a big smile lighting up her face. What I didn't expect was for my heart to skip a beat. She's in a long flowy shirt and a skirt that hugs all her curves. Her long, dark glossy hair is in a fancy braid, not a normal one. She doesn't look like she has a stitch of makeup on other than lip gloss.

"You always were glitter obsessed," I joke and reach for the glitter sprinkles.

"Daddy, who is that?" Skye says, pressing herself into my side.

"This is Calista, Cody's sister. And this is my daughter, Skye," I say, introducing the two.

"You look different than the photo on Nana's mantle." Skye carefully examines the woman in front of us.

She does look different. The photo was taken the year she graduated from high school. Calista has since filled out, and grown curves I'd kill to get my hands on. In the picture she's got on a boho style dress over her jeans. Usually she had on a t-shirt with her favorite pair of holey jeans.

"That photo was over ten years ago. You should have seen your dad back then," Calista laughs.

"I really like your hair. I have picture day tomorrow and I wish my daddy could do my hair like that, but he can't even braid," Skye says sadly.

"I'm learning!" I say, trying to defend myself.

"Dad, half my hair fell out when you put the hair tie in. It was a good try though," Skye says, patting my arm.

"Picture day is important. If it's okay with your dad, I can meet you before school and do your hair," Calista says. Then she freezes and gives me an apologetic look.

I can tell she feels like she overstepped, but the smile on my little girl's face is totally worth it.

"Can she? Please, Daddy?" Skye asks with all her exuberance and enthusiasm back.

"Are you sure it's not too much trouble? It would be around seven a.m.," I tell Calista.

"I mean, I live in the apartment over the shops the next block over, so that's not a big deal. You'd be surprised because I've switched to being more of a morning person over the years."

Calista used to be such a night owl. She would stay up well past midnight and hated getting up early for school or any other reason. As soon as she could drive and get coffee herself, she became a coffee addict. Her parents wouldn't let her make any at home because they tried to prevent her from getting dependent on it like her dad, but it didn't work.

"Can she please, Daddy?"

Skye is so excited I can't say no. "If you are willing, that would be amazing," I say.

We make arrangements for her to meet us in the elementary school's parking lot the next morning. I can feel Skye's excitement radiating. It will be good for her to have another woman in her life, I keep telling myself.

"I'm so excited. Daddy does try, but well, he's a boy, and boys don't do hair very good," Skye says to Calista like I'm not there, and they are best buddies wrapped up in a conversation.

"Come on, princess. Let's go find the rest of the stuff for your unicorn sundae." I say, pulling her attention from Calista, who shoots me a puzzled   look.

"I didn't know what a unicorn sundae was until your mom showed me. So, blame her when we are both in sugar comas tomorrow," I wink at her.

Then, taking Skye's hand, I lead her down the aisle, saying our goodbyes to Calista.

"I like her, Daddy. She is really pretty," Skye says when we are in the next aisle. "Did you grow up with her like you did with Uncle Cody?"

"Yeah, but she was older than us, so we didn't hang out with her much. Then she left for college before I was in high school," I tell her.

We find enough items to make a baby unicorn sundae as Skye is now calling it. Finally, we've found everything on our list, and we go home with the rest of our groceries.

"While I make dinner, why don't you take a shower and get ready for bed? That way, once you crash from the sugar high of the sundae, you will be ready to hop into bed," I say. I'm trying to get ahead of the drop she will have later.

She is so excited she doesn't fight me and runs upstairs to take a shower. It gives me a few minutes to get my head around running into Calista at the grocery store. It wouldn't have been so bad if we had run into each other, said hello, met Skye, and moved on. Regardless, she would have met Skye at dinner this weekend, but I was ready for that.

What I wasn't ready for was her and Skye to bond so instantly. And now for her to be involved with Skye, even if it's something as small as her hair for pictures. Right now, I need to lock away that part of my heart that still really wants a chance with her because it isn't an option. Not with her brother being my best friend. Her family is the only family my daughter knows. If something goes wrong, Skye and I lose that support in an instant, and I won't do that to my daughter.

Chapter 6

CALISTA

I don't think I thought this whole getting up early to do Skye's hair thing all the way through. Skye has such a sweet face that I just couldn't bring myself to say no to her. While I want to help, when my alarm went off at six-thirty this morning, I regretted it.

When I roll out of bed, thankfully, the smell of coffee is already filling my apartment. Whoever made scheduled AutoStart coffee machines deserves to live like royalty for the rest of his or her life.

Pouring my coffee, I go to the bathroom to get ready. If I wasn't meeting Kaylee later, I had every intention of showing up in pajamas, and throwing my hair up in a messy bun. But Kaylee really wanted to get together today after I do Skye's hair. She made me promise to bring coffee and breakfast from the bakery. Therefore, I have to get dressed and look presentable, so it doesn't get back to my parents, and I get a million questions. Or worse yet, rumors start about a breakup, I'm sick, or who knows what else because I'm walking around town in my pajamas.

Plus, there is no way I can meet up with a hot guy not looking my best. Even if it is my brother's best friend, who's way too young for me. That's okay. I can still enjoy the eye candy. There's nothing wrong with that, and my brothers never have to know.

I put on a hint of makeup, mascara, and lip gloss, mostly to give myself a natural look like I had yesterday. Then I pick out a fun flowy dress and a long sweater to go over it. After I put on some jewelry, I'm out the door. Since it's only a few blocks away, I decide to walk to the school, which will give me a chance to get enough of the view and enjoy the weirdly warm weather we are having this week.

With how quiet Main Street is this early, it's in stark contrast to the buzz all around the school area a few blocks off Main Street. Cars line the road and fill the parking lots. Buses drop kids off as they run to meet up with their friends. It brings up many childhood memories—mostly good.

I loved getting to school and seeing my friends and finding out what I'd missed in the way of gossip. Who started dating, who broke up, and who is fighting? Back then, I fed off it.

Finally, I spot Evan in the elementary school parking lot. He's in the same car he was in the night he answered my 911 call about the lady who had crashed into the mountain. I head over, and when I'm a few spots away, Skye jumps out of the car.

"You came! I'm so excited. I brought pretty much everything we have for my hair, which isn't a lot. But Dad promised to take me shopping for more and to take some online tutorials to learn!" Skye says, holding a small bin in one hand and a hairbrush in the other.

"Alright, let's see what we are working with," I tell her.

Taking the bin from her, I place it on the trunk of the car. Then I pull out a few hair ties and take the brush to work on the braid. Skye holds perfectly still as I put her in each position. Even though Evan watches quietly what I do, I can tell before I even hit the halfway point that he's overwhelmed, but he is still paying attention.

When I'm done, Skye jumps into the front passenger seat of the car and pulls the mirror down, checking her hair at every possible angle she can.

"I love it! It's going to be the best picture day photo ever! Thank you so much!" She rushes over, throws her arms around my waist, and hugs me tight.

At first, I'm stunned. But when I look at Evan, who has a huge smile on his face, I wrap Skye in a bear hug.

"Let me walk her in, and we can go to the bakery and get some coffee," he says as Skye grabs her backpack from the car.

"Oh, you don't have to," I say, ready to walk to the bakery myself.

"I insist as a thank you for this. Please wait while I walk her in. Sit in the car, stay warm," he says, staring at me, waiting for me to agree.

"Okay," I nod and sit down in the passenger seat to wait for him.

While he's gone, I check my phone for texts and scroll through social media. He's not gone very long, and when he gets in the car, he shoots me one of his smiles, and my heart flutters.

During the drive over to the bakery, we're silent. It's comfortable and easy. After finding a parking spot right out front, we walk into the bakery. He is the perfect gentleman and holds the door open for me. We each get coffee and a pastry and grab a table in the back corner of the shop.

"Have you seen the distillery yet?" he asks, breaking the ice.

"I drove by, and it was pretty busy, so I didn't stop."

"It's always busy. You just have to go on in. I'm sure the guys can't wait to show it to you. They have done a great job with it," he says, grinning.

It's obvious from his demeanor that he's both excited and proud of them.

"I'll brave it one day next week once I'm done unpacking," I say.

Even though I'm pushing off seeing it and know I need to go over there, I crave some time to decompress and adjust to this move. Hell, I agreed to help them with it, but for right now, I need some more time to adjust to all the changes.

"You settling in okay?" he asks.

"Yeah, just kind of taking it easy. I'm going to spend some time with Kaylee today. Maybe do a bit of shopping later. It's been forever since I've had time off. I want to enjoy it a little before jumping back into things."

"I get that. But I meant what I said. If you need anything, you reach out and let me know. I'm always happy to help," he says, finishing up his coffee.

"I will. But so far, I'm just kind of lying low."

"Good. Thanks for taking this time with me, but I'm going to have to cut our time short. I need to get to the station. Hopefully, today I'll be getting some info on a case I'm working on," he says, taking the last bite of his Danish.

"Anything exciting?" I ask and watch a hint of something cross his face. Guilt, maybe, or sadness?

"Just the usual. But I can't talk much about it," he says, standing up.

"I understand." Joining him, I toss out my now-empty coffee. "I'm going to grab coffee and breakfast for Kaylee before I leave." I nod toward the counter.

"Okay, be safe, and thank you again for doing Skye's hair."

Awkwardly, he reaches out and gives me a hug. His scent wraps around me, and his arms around me are comforting. I take a step back. The last thing I need is to obsess over his scent and his hard body and his muscles and... I need to stop thinking right now.

He strides confidently to the door, and I watch him as he heads to the station. After placing another order for coffee and some muffins, I walk across the street to my place and get my car to go to Kaylee's place south of town.

When I get there, she is sitting on the front porch, wrapped in a blanket. She jumps up and greets me as I step onto the porch.

"Oh, my god! Coffee with Detective Greer? Tell me everything!" She gushes, taking the coffee and pulling me inside.

"How the heck do you know about that before I even get here?" I ask, shocked, before sitting on the couch with her.

"Have you really forgotten what it's like to live in Whiskey River? Maisie called when she saw you. Her living room looks right over the bakery, you know. She was trying to see what I knew, which was, of course, less than her. Which, as your best friend, just isn't right!"

"It wasn't planned. I ran into them at the grocery store last night, and his daughter loved my hair, and one thing led to another, and I agreed to meet them at the school to do her hair. He insisted on getting me coffee as a thank you. We talked about my brother and you. Nothing fancy," I tell her as she digs into the bag of muffins I brought.

"Still, a small text could have given me a leg up on the gossip!" she says, smiling.

"If there is a next time, I will try to remember."

"That's all I'm asking for." She sighs, "Calvin and I broke up."

I try to muster up some fake emotion like shock or sadness, but I'm not sure if it's believable.

Actually, I'm glad they're not together anymore. I never liked the guy, mostly because he checked out other women and didn't treat her well when he was with her. She soaked up any ounce of affection he bestowed on her, though it wasn't much, even from the beginning.

"I want to say sorry, but I'm honestly glad. What happened?" I ask.

"I should have listened to you. But I found out he was using drugs, and when I confronted him, he was all, 'Who the fuck are you to judge me, ugly bitch.' That's when I ended it, and he took what stuff he could carry that night, and I sent him a photo of me burning the rest in the backyard last night. It was very cathartic," she says, shocking the hell out of me.

"First, good for you! Second, who should have called who? And third, you have plenty of time to find a good guy," I encourage her.

She just rolls her eyes but doesn't say anything.

Kaylee is younger thane by almost five years. She was super smart in school, skipped two grades, and was always more mature than the kids in my own grade. Somehow, we just bonded.

"I know. It's the waiting part I hate," she says.

"Don't I know it? But it's better to be alone than stuck with a mooching idiot," I say.

"Don't I know it," she sighs.

Chapter 7
EVAN

All I have been able to think about is the coffee I had with Calista yesterday. She is so easy to talk to, but then I had to go and make it awkward with that hug. Not to mention that everyone in town talked about it all day, to the point Cody even texted me to ask what was going on. When I told him about her doing Skye's hair and the coffee as a thank you, he blew it off.

It's too bad the rest of the town can't do that. Judy kept asking me questions like she was interrogating a suspect, waiting to see if my answers changed. They didn't. Even Maggie had heard about it by the time I picked Skye up from her house yesterday and thought it was so sweet of her to meet Skye and help out.

"Hey man, I saw that new commercial with Skye's mom in it," my co-worker Rick says.

Rick is older than me by a few years. Even though he is milking the desk job like no one's business, he is one of the best people to investigate using the internet. He can dig and find things that are instrumental in solving cases.

"Yeah, but we don't keep up with any of her appearances. But you know that," I remind him.

When Skye's mom walked away from her, I cut her from our lives all the way. The town knows what happened and keeps up with her career, but we haven't even seen a single commercial. Skye has zero interest in doing so, and when she does, then that's a bridge I will cross.

"It's been seven years, and this commercial is the biggest gig with the most lines she's gotten. I'd say karma is taking care of her," Rick says before he walks off.

Brittney had dreams of being a movie star, and she surely thought she'd be a household name seven years later. She has been able to land some soap shows and a handful of commercials, but she has left us alone, and that's all I want, and I am happy about it.

"Is there anything new on that drug case?" I ask Judy, who tends to hear things before they are even official.

"We might get some info on it later today. But I want to talk about the BBQ cook-off. You are entering, right?" Whiskey River is like all small towns, and we have a bunch of festivals and events to draw people in and make the town some money. The BBQ Competition is one that has been around for a long time.

While it does have a contest, that is a small part of the event. There will be craft booths, sales tables, and an entire section of tasting booths from about any business within a fifty-mile radius. All the stores participate in offering special foods or sales for the event. There are decorations on Main Street, posters are up, and ads on the radio. It's a big affair and a moneymaker for everyone.

Every year since she was three, Skye and I have entered the competition with my dad's recipe. It's been more of a fun thing for us to do together. I didn't care much about winning or losing, but two years ago, we won third place. Then, last year, the police station sponsored our booth, and we won second.

Since the station is sponsoring us again, I'm not sure I have a choice whether to enter or not. But how could I possibly say no? In addition, we will be selling my bottled BBQ sauce. The station will vote on which charity any prize money will go to, and from the flurry around the station, nominations are rolling in.

"Of course. Skye is looking forward to it, maybe more than I am," I say.

"Well, this year, you have a bigger kitchen to work with, but if you need help, you let me know. I am happy to rally the troops," she says, walking off.

This year there will be more competition than ever before. It just keeps getting bigger. Since Cody and his brothers have the distillery open, they are using one of their whiskeys to make a BBQ sauce. If they place in the competition, they have bragging rights and can use it to help sell the sauce at their retail store and restaurant they are planning on opening.

I want them to place, and I want to raise money for charity. Regardless of whether we place or not, people will be buying our BBQ, and hopefully, our sauce. But it's more important for Cody to actually get in the top three.

Since I'm waiting for information from another cop on this drug case, I have some downtime. Normally, I'd clean out my email or catch up with Cody. Today, though, I'm reaching for my phone and find myself texting Calista.

Me: I wanted to thank you again for doing Skye's hair. She got many compliments.

I send it thinking I won't hear anything back right away, if at all. We aren't friends that text like this, but something in me wants to have that little thread of connection with her. I'm starting to clean out my email when my phone goes off. When I realize it's from her, I almost drop it on the floor.

Calista: I'm so glad she liked it. You know, I'm always happy to help. It seems like such a small thing, but it's a big deal when they are that young. Believe me, I remember.

Me: Well, she has named you her personal hair stylist from here on out, so be ready. The school picture circuit is more than just the yearbook photo nowadays.

Calista: Oh yeah?

Me: Yes, they have the yearbook photo, parents' photos for purchase, a class photo, a photo of the entire grade, plus photos for each activity, and all are shot on different days.

Calista: That sounds like pictures are a big event. Well, I am happy to meet her and do her hair for each photo. But you should look up some video tutorials and learn to do some yourself. There are some really easy ones out there.

Me: We have tried. I promise I'm hopeless. I can't even get a ponytail done right. Your mom has tried to teach me many times and has called me a lost cause.

Calista: Oh, it must be true because Mom is the authority on all things hair.

Even through the text, I can hear her sarcasm, and it makes me smile.

"Who has you smiling like a love-struck teenager?" Rick asks, walking by my desk again.

"No one. Mind your business," I tell him, but I don't even bother wiping the smile off my face.

"Well, when you are done, there is something in here you will want to see," he says, setting a folder in front of me.

When I nod, he leaves, but I turn back to my phone.

> **Me:** In this case, I think it's true. I will let Skye know you volunteered to do her hair on the next picture day.

> **Calista:** Good. We'll have to pick out something ahead of time. Then, she and I will talk over family dinner.

> **Me:** Sounds like a plan. She will be excited. But I have to get back to work.

> **Calista:** Be safe.

> **Me:** Always am.

Something about her wanting me to be safe warms my heart. I know it's probably more for her brother's benefit than hers, but either way, I like it.

I put my phone away and grab the folder Rick set down.

Flipping it open, I start reading some reports related to my drug case here in town. It looks like after some surveillance, we finally got an address on where they are buying the drugs. Why does this address look familiar? I can't put my finger on it, so I pull the address up on my computer, and when I see the street view, it hits me.

The address is so familiar because it's Calista's best friend's house. That can't be right. I know Kaylee isn't selling drugs.

Right?

There is always a buzz when the warrant comes in and you are putting the wheels in motion to do a raid. We do it maybe once or twice a year, and it's a big event that the entire station gets in on. Normally, I feel prepared, but this time, my gut is churning.

I can't put my finger on it, but I get a feeling this isn't going to go smoothly. Though I don't share my thoughts with anyone. I might just be feeling out of sorts because I don't know what to expect, and with it being Kaylee's place, it's personal. We know this is the time to catch them. The deals have been happening at this place twice a week, between ten in the morning and two in the afternoon like clockwork for over a month now.

Another reason for my gut feeling is how do I break this to Calista if Kaylee is involved in any way? As of now, I have no proof that she is, and I hope she isn't, but this is her place, so there is still a possibility.

"Alright, let's roll. You all know your jobs," Chief Barton says.

Only a few guys are hanging back at the station to take on anything that comes up that can't be put off for a few hours. Judy and the other assistants are staying as well. Otherwise, the rest of us get our vests on and head out to our vehicles one by one, random formation. We are all going different ways there, so we won't draw attention to anyone who is on their way there too.

After we all partnered up, Rick is at my side. I like him, but he isn't one to fill the silence with chit-chat, so we both concentrate on the task at hand on our way over to the house.

"Alright, months of paperwork leading up to this. Let's shut it down," he says as we park at the big empty lot down the road we are using as a meeting spot and wait for orders to enter.

Everything is done according to the book. We move in and cover all the exits, and then a group of us, me included, head up to the door. My job is to go in and get the evidence while at the same time having the men's backs who are going to bust in.

There are two cars in the driveway. Kaylee's and her ex's. I thought they broke up, at least according to the intel we have aka the Whiskey River gossip tree, but they could have gotten back together. Only I know that isn't true when we get up to the door, and I can hear them screaming. We pause for just a moment to listen.

"We broke up, so you don't get to come and go from my house at will anymore, Calvin," Kaylee yells.

"I said I just came to get the rest of my stuff. Lord, what is your problem? Aren't you supposed to be at work?" Calvin says, and I'm pretty sure he rolled his eyes with that one, judging by the tone of his voice.

"I told you I burned that shit. And I came home because I wasn't feeling good. Not that it matters, it's my house! I took your key. How the fuck did you even get in?"

"I made a copy and kept it at my place after I thought I lost my keys. What is the big deal?"

"The big deal is we broke up, and I come home to find you in my house. This is breaking and entering and burglary, since none of this is yours anymore. I'm calling the cops!"

"The fuck you are!" he yells.

That's when the Chief gives the signal, and the guys burst through the door. Both Calvin and Kaylee scream because neither was expecting us. Kaylee freezes and puts her hands up, fear evident on her face. The anger from a moment ago, long gone.

Calvin, on the other hand, tries to make a run for it out the back door. One of the guys gets Kaylee in handcuffs and out the front door while we go after Calvin. A few of the other men clear the rest of the house.

Calvin didn't plan well. The back door leads out to a covered porch and a fenced-in backyard, where we have men stationed and ready for him. He tries to dodge them, but when he makes a hard turn to the right, he runs right into Rick and me. As we tackle him to the ground, he fights hard. It's clear he's on something because he's strong for a skinny guy who plays video games all day. He slips from Rick's grasp, and his arms flail. When he flips over, I use my body to hold him down while Rick and another guy get him in the handcuffs.

The next thing I know, a gunshot goes off, and people are screaming, but it sounds far away. Then pain erupts all over my body, and my vision closes in. I can't move my hands or feet, and then everything goes black.

Chapter 8

Calista

I 'm on my way to Kaylee's house. She texted me saying she was leaving work because she was not feeling well. She asked me to pick up some stuff at the store for her, and I also grabbed everything I need to make her favorite chicken noodle soup. We can hang out on the couch and watch movies while she rests.

Only when I turn down her street, it's pure chaos. Cop cars line the street, and people are yelling. I pull onto the road just past her driveway and get out of the car to see what is going on. What I see causes me to panic and run toward the house.

"Calista, you can't go in there," Chief Barton says.

The man should be retired by now. He and my dad went to school together, and he's known me my whole life.

"What is going on?" I ask.

"It's a drug raid," he says.

"Kaylee and drugs?" I say in shock.

"Kaylee!" I shout.

"Calista, I'm fine!" Kaylee yells from the other side of the street, wrapped in a blanket.

"Then what the hell is going on?" I ask, running over to her.

"I got home, and Calvin was in my house. We got into a fight, and the next thing I knew, the cops were busting in. They say he's been selling drugs from my house while I've been at work."

"Seriously?" I ask.

"Yeah, they brought me out here, but Calvin tried to run out the back. They were chasing him, but I don't know if they got him or not."

"What the fuck," I say shocked.

"Yeah, I guess it's been going on for a while. I didn't see anything when I got home, so I didn't even think anything of it. I was getting dizzy from all the yelling, and I wanted him gone, but he wasn't leaving. At this point I'm thankful they haven't kept me in hand-cuffs," she says, resting her head on my shoulder.

We watch the cops all moving in and out of her house and in her front yard until a gunshot goes off. It's as if time stops and everyone freezes. There's silence and then we can hear everyone's radio go off.

"Officer down! I repeat, Officer down!" A voice yells through the radio, and people run into the house.

"I have to help," I say, moving toward the house.

"Go!" Kaylee yells.

I look at Chief Barton. "I'm an ER nurse. Get me in there and let me help until the ambulance arrives."

"I can't... the suspect hasn't been..." he doesn't finish the words before his radio goes off again.

"Suspect in custody," the voice says.

Then Chief looks at me and nods.

"Backyard," he says, and I take off running, going over bullet protocol in my head as I get into the backyard.

"Move. She's an ER nurse," Chief says behind me.

When the guys move, I see Evan lying on the ground with blood on his shirt and pants. I freeze for just a moment before all my training kicks in and I drop to my knees beside him and try to find the bullet hole to stop the bleeding.

Ripping open his vest, I see most of the blood coming from his shoulder, so I work on opening his shirt.

"I need a towel, shirt, or gauze," I call out as I confirm he's been shot in his right shoulder.

Another officer runs up, opens a metal box, and starts handing me gauze packs. The other men keep opening them as I pack his wound.

"Evan, can you hear me?" I talk to him, but I can tell he has no idea what's going on. He moans when I speak.

"Ambulance is two minutes out," Chief says.

"He's going to need to be airlifted to Helena. The hospital here isn't set up for this kind of surgery unless something has changed," I say.

"The field where we met would allow a safe helicopter landing," another man says.

"I'm on it," yet another shouts.

I don't bother looking up to see who is talking. I keep my eyes on Evan.

Increasing my pressure on the wound, I'm attempting to stop as much bleeding as possible.

Evan groans again.

"Stay with me, Evan. Help is on the way. Please stay with me." My emotions are threatening to take over. I can't have that happening. I've worked with people I knew before and have been able to keep my emotions at bay. My emotions have never run amok before while on the job.

"Medics are here," Chief says, and everyone else moves out of the way.

Shaking my emotions off, I focus by giving the medics the information on what I know and on what I did. They have more equipment and can get his wound more stabilized. Once he's on the stretcher, I start to follow them out to the ambulance when the Chief stops me.

"This is something your brother should hear in person. Help them set up care for Skye and then meet us at the hospital. You would be doing me a huge favor by letting your family know. Give me your number and I will call if I hear anything before you get to the hospital," Chief says as Kaylee comes running up to me.

"Okay. Umm, is she free to go?" I ask, hugging Kaylee.

"Yes, but other than the hospital, no leaving town. We will have a lot of follow-up questions," he says.

"I'm not leaving her side, so I'll be with her for a few days," Kaylee says.

The Chief nods and walks off.

"Come on. I'll drive you to the distillery. You can talk to Cody in person. Call your parents on the way," Kaylee orders, taking my car keys from me.

Grateful that she's taking charge, I follow her to my car. "Are you sure you feel up to driving?" I ask.

"Maybe it's the adrenaline, but I'm feeling much better," she says.

I pull out my phone and as we turn off her road, I watch the medevac copter land a few streets over.

Knowing it's better to let Dad tell my mom, I give him a call hoping he's around.

"Good morning, sweetheart. I was just thinking about checking with you to see if you wanted to grab coffee."

"Daddy," I choke out, and there is no hiding that something is wrong.

"Are you okay?" he asks urgently.

"I am. Evan's been shot. They are airlifting him to Helena now. I was there when it happened. They were arresting Kaylee's ex for selling drugs. It was a big drug bust."

"Do your brothers know?" he asks.

"No, I'm going to go tell Cody now and take him with us to the hospital. Can you and Mom get Skye from school?"

"Of course. We will not tell her anything is wrong until we know more. How bad is it?"

"He was shot in the shoulder. I was able to stop the bleeding, so I don't think it hit anything major, but I have no way of knowing as he was really out of it."

"Shit, okay. I will tell your mom. Go and let me know as soon as you hear anything," Dad says as we pull into the distillery.

"Okay, I'm at the distillery now. I love you."

"Love you too, sweet pea," Dad says softly.

After I hang up and compose myself, Kaylee and I enter the distillery. This isn't exactly how I thought my first time seeing the distillery would go, and honestly, I'm not seeing a single detail. I'm completely focused on Cody.

"Hey Kaylee," Cody says, smiling happily until he sees me, and his face drops.

"What's wrong?" He rushes over to me.

"Cody, Evan's been shot. I was there, and they were airlifting him to Helena. We need to go now!"

"Fuck!" he yells, and my brothers Drew and Kaiden come running.

"What's wrong?" my oldest brother, Drew, asks.

Kaylee fills them in, and Cody turns to me.

"Skye?" he asks. Then pulls out his phone while going out the front door.

"Mom and Dad are picking her up from school," I say.

"They will want to go to the hospital, too. We'll close this afternoon, and I'll call Colt. And we will relieve Mom and Dad so they can join you," Kaiden says.

Colt is our youngest brother and a bit of a wild one, but he takes family seriously.

"Mom will have to pick Skye up, as only she and I are on the approved list," Cody says.

"We got this. Go! Call with anything you need," Drew says.

"Let's take my truck. I'll drive. Leave your keys with Kaiden and we will get it back to Mom and Dad's," Cody says.

I hand Kaiden my keys, and both he and Drew give me a hug before I follow Cody out to his truck.

Kaylee and I both get in the backseat, and Kaylee wraps her arms around me. My heart is in my throat and I'm glad for the comfort Kaylee's providing me.

"You ever have to work on someone you knew before?" Cody asks as we leave Whiskey River city limits and make the climb up the mountain.

"Yes, but this is hitting differently. He feels like family."

"Now, what exactly happened?" Cody asks.

We spend the rest of the drive telling him the story, hoping it makes time pass faster.

Chapter 9

Evan

Fuck, I knew I needed a new bed, but I haven't ever woken up with every inch of my body hurting like this. When I try to move, my body feels like it's being weighed down with lead. I groan and try to open my eyes, but it's so bright that I shut them again.

"Hey, take it easy. Cody, can you turn the lights down?" The sweetest voice in the world says.

Calista.

What is she doing here? Where am I?I try to open my eyes again, and it's not as bright. When I turn my head toward Calista's voice, pain shoots down my arm.

"Hey, don't move. What do you need?" she asks.

"Where am I?" I croak.

Before she answers, she lifts a straw to my mouth, and I drink. The ice-cold water feels great going down my throat.

"In the hospital in Helena. Do you remember what happened?" she asks.

I think for a moment. What do I remember? We were raiding Kaylee's place. There was arguing at the door. Calvin ran and…. Fuck, the asshole shot me.

"I was shot. Don't remember much after that," I say.

"This girl saved your life," Rick says, stepping up beside her.

"What?" I ask.

"Kaylee went home from work sick, so I was just getting to her place to check on her. When I got there, it was chaos with cops running around. Then we heard a gunshot. I raced back, not knowing it was you. By the way, you are never allowed to scare me like that again," she says, squeezing my hand.

I hadn't even realized until now she was holding it.

"I'll grab a nurse," Rick says.

Cody takes his place on the bed. "Hey, you know this is the day we always feared. I'm glad you're okay," he says.

"You and me both," I say.

"Mom and Dad are in the waiting room. I'm going to go let them know you are okay," he says and leaves Calista and me alone.

"Skye?" I ask.

"Mom picked her up from school, and Drew, Colt, and Kaiden stayed with her at their house. They built this elaborate fort in the living room. We haven't told her yet. We didn't want to stress her out too much," she says.

"She is a lot for them to handle for more than a night. Plus, she will want to be back in her own bed, and she has a project due at the end of the week, and it's in her room," my mind races.

"That's no problem. I can go get all her stuff and stay with Mom and Dad to help out," she says.

That calms me enough that I can smile at her. There's a soft knock on the door, which pulls my attention from her. Her parents walk in, greeting me.

"I'm so glad you are awake!" Maggie comes over, takes my hand from Calista, and holds it between hers. "You gave us quite a scare. While it's always a possibility, we thought the chances were so slim in Whiskey River!"

Don wraps his arm around his wife's shoulders and smiles.

"I can't wait to hear all about it. Did they tell you that Skye is with us?"

"I just told him," Calista says from the back of the room.

"Do you want us to bring her up to see you?" Maggie asks.

"I want to hold her, but I don't want her to see me like this. This isn't what I want her to picture every time I go off to work. Do you think we can video call her?"

"Of course! I don't think Cody is leaving your side, and Calista has been here the whole time, too. So we can set it up, I'm sure," Maggie says.

Calista has been here the whole time? Why does that thought make my heart race? I'm sure it has to do with Cody being here, too. Cody's here, and being it's her brother, she's probably here to support him.

"Well, I just wanted to pop in and see you with my own eyes. Since you seem to be in good hands, we are going to go home and talk with Skye," Maggie says.

"I will be here. Just call me, and we can set up a video call," Cody says, walking back in.

They give me an awkward hug and leave as Rick and the nurse walk in.

"I called the Chief so he could let the guys know you are up. He's been processing a ton of paperwork and getting Calvin booked," Rick says.

"Did you guys catch him?" I ask.

"Yep. Calvin was being held until we found out how you did to see what his official charges would be. I'm sure he will be happy to have his charges dropped from murder to assault of a police officer on top of all the drug charges," Rick says.

"I'm glad you got him," I say.

"Well, I'm heading out. I have a ton of paperwork too. Calista, you got the Chief's number. Keep him updated, yeah?" Rick says.

"I will," she says, hugging Rick.

"Okay, pause the shop talk. How are we feeling, Detective?" The nurse asks after taking my vitals.

"Like I've been shot."

"Well, you are due for more pain meds, so I will go get those. Did they tell you about your injuries?" she asks.

"No," I say with a slight cough as my throat is so dry.

I don't even have to ask Calista if she has the water there because the straw is already to my lips.

"Well, you were lucky. Even though you were shot, it missed any major veins. You did have quite a bit of blood loss. After you were rushed into surgery, they removed the bullet and repaired your shoulder. It will take some time to heal and then some physical therapy, but you are expected to make a good recovery. We will know more once the swelling is down. Also, you have a sprained wrist and a sprained ankle, lots of bruises, and a mild concussion. You have a long road ahead of you," she finishes.

"How long will I be here?"

"A few days, most likely. We want to make sure you are healing and that there are no adverse effects from the concussion. When you are released, you won't be able to be on your own. For the first few weeks, you will need help because you can't use crutches, and you can't walk on your leg."

Great, I can't even think about making those arrangements considering how much my head hurts right now.

The nurse leaves, and Calista comes back to my side, taking my hand again.

"Calista can stay with you when you get out," Cody says.

"What?" The thought of Calista in my place sets my head spinning.

"She is experienced at things like this. Skye likes her, so that's not a problem. You know she will love having another female around. Even better, Calista knows what to watch for, so the chances they will let you out earlier are higher," Cody says.

"I'm happy to do it. The distillery can wait," Calista says.

"I don't want to be a burden."

"You aren't. You are family and this is what family does," Cody says.

I just nod as the nurse comes back in and gives me a dose of what I assume are pain meds through the IV.

"I'm going to go to your place, geta bag together for Skye, and check on my brothers. I will be back tomorrow. Let me know if you want me to bring you anything," Calista says.

"Make sure to grab Skye's unicorn stuffie. She can't sleep without it. Though she will try hard to convince you that she needs to wear a fancy dress to school. She doesn't. Jeans are fine," I say.

"We got this. This isn't our first rodeo with her. She will be fine, I promise," Cody says before turning to Calista. "Can you stay a little longer? I have a few calls to make."

"No problem, take your time," she says.

"You sure? Do you need anything?" Cody asks.

"Nope. I'm good," she says, and she hugs Cody before he leaves.

"Are you sure you are okay staying with me when I get out?" I ask her when it's just the two of us.

"I promise I am. Actually, I'm looking forward to spending some time with Skye."

I can feel the drugs working, and things get a bit fuzzy. But one thought keeps circling in my head.

I hope you don't see me as family.

Chapter 10

CALISTA

Evan's words still echo in my head as I head back to Whiskey River.

I hope you don't see me as family.

"I don't think he realized he said it out loud. He was drifting off because of the pain meds and he was asleep right after he said it." I tell Kaylee, who is riding home with me. Cody had me take his truck since Mom and Dad left before me. Kaylee had stuck around and was waiting with us, too.

That was the first thing I told her when I got in the car, and she screamed so loud I almost crashed the truck.

"I really think that man likes you more than a sister. The way people described how he was looking at you in the coffee shop," she sighs with a smile.

"Oh, you know how people over-exaggerate." I dismiss it because it's true.

"Talk to him about it," she shrugs, like it's the easiest thing in the world.

"Oh yeah. Hey Evan, while you are healing from being shot in my best friend's backyard, remember what you said when you were high on pain meds? What did you mean by that?" I say in a sarcastic tone.

"Fine. Fine. I get it. Just give it time and pay attention. If he likes you, you will be able to tell, especially since you guys will live together for a few weeks," she says with a smirk.

It's then her phone rings.

"I think it is the station," she says, answering the call.

I only hear her side, but it's a bunch of 'okay' and 'seriously' until she says, "Well, when can I get back in?" Then there's another pause.

"Can I at least take my car?" Then another pause.

"Fine."

She hangs up the phone and tosses her face into her hands in frustration.

"I can't get into my house because it's a crime scene. They had to pause the search until they heard about Evan, and they are still going through everything. The Chief packed me a bag of clothes. I can pick up my bag at the station, and I can get my car. But I just can't go into the house."

"Okay, well, that's fine. You can stay at my place. I won't be there, and there is plenty of food. It's right downtown. If I keep my car with my parents, you can have my parking space. I will let my landlord know."

"Did you hear me? The Chief packed a bag of my clothes!" she squeals.

"Okay, spell it out like I'm a toddler. It's been a really long day," I say.

"He. Touched. My. Underwear." She over pronounces each word.

"Okay, I can fix that." I take the next right and pull into the closest superstore. "Let's get you some clean ones."

We get out of the truck, and she hugs me tightly. We're on the same wavelength, which is why we're such good friends.

I hate big stores like this because we go in for one thing and walk out with eleven items an hour later. Sure enough, that's exactly what happened. Once we're back in the car, I check my phone before I pull out of the parking lot. There's a text from a number I don't have saved.

Unknown: Hey, this is Emelie. We met at the hospital when we visited Evan. Your brother gave me your number. I hope that's okay.

Emelie and her husband, Axel, arrived right as I was leaving. She gave me a hug and welcomed me home. I don't know her all that well, but she seems sweet and caring. When she suggested I get together with her and the other girls, I said okay, but we didn't work out any details as I had to go.

Me: No problem, it's good I have your number. And I know we'd talked briefly at the hospital about getting together, and I'd love to meet up. Once he gets out of the hospital, I'll be staying with Evan until he is back on his feet. So, we'll have to play it by ear.

Emelie: Sounds good! I am going to hold you to that! Save my number and let me know if you need help with anything. I can stock his freezer and I'm great at cleaning and laundry!

Me: Wow! Music to my ears!

"Who's that?" Kaylee asks, as I set my phone down and start driving.

"Some of Evan's friends were visiting when I was leaving. His friend's wife got my number from Cody and texted to say if I needed help to let her know. She said she'd cook or clean and wanted to get together once he was feeling better," I told her.

"That's nice. You do need to make friends other than me, as much as I hate to share you."

"Girl, if I meet up with her and her friends, you best believe you are coming with me." I reach over and squeeze her hand, and she gives me a teary smile.

The rest of the way home, we talk about anything other than the events that happened today. It's almost too much. I take Kaylee right to her house and she gets her car, and I give her my housekey.

"I'll be by to pack my bag, but make yourself at home," I tell her, giving her a hug. Then I plug Evan's address, which Cody gave me, into the GPS.

Cody told me Evan had just moved into this place right before I came home and to expect things to still be inboxes. Otherwise, I know nothing but the address and the code to the door.

It's a short drive into the mountains. Even though it's fairly isolated, it's not too hard to find. Motion lights kick on as I pull up in front of the house, and from what I can see, the place looks beautiful. I check my surroundings before stepping out of the car. My dad always taught me never to be too careful in the woods around here.

I get to the door and put the code in. The door opens, and I turn on the light and gasp. The cabin is magazine level stunning. It has an open concept with a gigantic stone fireplace, and a kitchen that makes me jealous. The place looks mostly set up with just a few boxes in the corner, but the walls are pretty bare.

Going upstairs, I easily find Skye's room. Her unicorn stuffie is on the unmade bed, so I make the bed, pick up the unicorn, and go in search of a bag in her closet. Not finding what I'm looking for, I go to Evan's room and look in his closet. Since I keep my luggage on the top shelf of my closet, I figure that's a good place to start looking.

As soon as I walk into his room, I smell his cologne. His bed is made, and everything seems to be in its place. I want to snoop, but I know I shouldn't, especially since this man is lying in a hospital bed right now. Instead, I move to his closet, and sure enough, I find two duffle bags on the top shelf above a row of his uniforms.

One bag is all black, and the other is black and pink. Without a doubt in my mind, the pink one must be Skye's, so I grab it, putting the unicorn safely in the side pocket of the duffle. Then, going to her dresser,

I pack everything she'll need for the rest of the week. I make sure to grab her stuff from the bathroom, too, and load it into my car. Taking one more trip back inside, I make sure everything is turned off and locked securely before I leave and go to my place.

Also, I want to check on Kaylee and make sure she is settled in, and I need to pack my own bag before heading over to Mom and Dad's.

Once I'm at my parents' house, it's all hands-on board to come up with a plan to help with Skye and Evan. Cody is to stay at the hospital with Evan, and Mom is on drop-off and pickup duty with Skye. Drew, Colt, and Kaiden will work during the day and take turns, with one of them coming home each night to help out. I am free during the day, but on Skye duty at night. Per Mom's insistence, Dad will be back and forth at the hospital checking on Cody and Evan.

When I pull into the parking area at my apartment, Kaylee's car is there, so I walk up the stairs, knock, and then open the door. Before I even get to call out for her, I can hear her crying from my bedroom.

"It's me," I call, closing the door and dropping my purse to check on her.

I find her lying on my bed, curled up and sobbing. So, I do what any best friend would do and crawl into bed beside her, pull her into my arms and let her cry. I don't bother asking what is wrong. Whenever she wants to talk, she knows I'm here. But right now, I can tell she just needs a good cry to get it all out of her system.

I'm thinking that the day is catching up with her. All in a matter of one forty-eight period, she broke up with her boyfriend, had her house raided, a friend got shot, and then she got displaced. That would take a toll on anyone.

"Not only does the Chief have questions for me, but they also consider me a person of interest in the drug dealings. Apparently, they didn't quite believe that it was happening in my house, and I had no clue. I never, not once, found drugs in the house. In this day and age, all these strangers coming and going are a huge red flag. How could I be so unaware?" she sniffles.

"Let's not panic just yet. They are in the early stages of putting everything together. I'm sure they put the case on pause until they knew what was going on with Evan. Give it a few more days. I bet they'll realize you have nothing to do with all this once they get through all the evidence they've collected."

"Maybe? I guess?" She says, wiping her face.

"Then I know a damn good lawyer who will help you out," I tell her.

"Yeah, I should talk to Jack and see what his advice is with all this," she says, sitting up.

Hugging her, I start packing my bag. "That would be a good idea. You are close enough here that you can walk down there and enjoy the fresh air."

"I wish you could stay here with me," she sighs dramatically.

"Me too, but Skye will be so scared. Plus, my mom will need help. Can you picture my brothers being in charge of a seven-year-old for more than a few hours? She'd live on cake and ice cream and never sleep!" I laugh.

This makes Kaylee laugh, which encourages me.

"I guess I can let you go for a good cause," she says, hugs me again, and helps me pack my bag.

After we chatted for a while, I couldn't stall anymore and go to my parents' house. It's already been a long day, and I am ready to sleep, but there is a little girl who will need a lot of comfort tonight.

Chapter 11

Evan

I really hope the hospital plans to let me go soon because it wasn't so bad here on the first day. On day two, I started to really miss my daughter, and the video calls weren't helping. But now, here's day three, and it's the longest she and I have been apart. I am more than ready to go.

Cody hasn't left my side, and I am so grateful for it. I can't imagine being left here alone with my own thoughts. But even with his company, I'm still going a bit stir-crazy, so when Rick walks in the door, I am relieved, to say the least. Now, I can find out what is going on with Calvin's case.

"I'm going to head out and get some non-hospital food and let you guys talk. I'll smuggle you some food back in." Cody stands and shakes Rick's hand.

"I'll stay with him until you get back," Rick says, and Cody nods.

We watch Cody go before Rick turns to me.

"How are you feeling?" he asks.

"Like I've been shot and stuck in a hospital for days on end." I give my standard reply, but he sees right through it.

"How are you really"? He asks, pulling up the chair.

"Well, I miss my daughter, and I'm ready to get out of here. While I hate the pain meds I'm on and how they make me feel not like myself, I hate the pain when I don't take them." I give him full honesty. He was there when it happened. I owe him at least that.

"Yeah," he says. "I had my appendix removed, and I hated the IV pain meds, but the pills they gave me when I went home didn't make me feel doped up. So, I hope that's the case with you, too."

"Let's hope. What is going on with Calvin's case?" I ask.

"They are still going through the house."

"What? Why is it taking so long, and where is Kaylee staying?"

"Well, you were shot with an illegal weapon. Her house was being used as a place to sell drugs, yet we have found nothing. Kaylee is staying at Calista's place while Calista is staying at her parents' helping with Skye."

"Calvin did a stupid thing, but he's smart. Did you get a warrant to check his place?" I ask.

"Yes, that took longer than it should have. Once you were shot, everything stopped until we knew you were okay. Right now, the guys are over there searching his house, but I haven't heard any updates."

"I still don't understand why they are so fixated on Kaylee's place if they didn't find anything," I wonder out loud. What am I missing? Are the drugs making things too hazy?

"Well, think about it," Rick says. "Everyone has cameras these days, fancy doorbells, or security measures. She didn't. Why? Also, you are telling me that with all the strangers in and out, she noticed nothing? Some of the guys think she is hiding something. I don't know if she is anything other than too trusting. It's not clear."

"Or it's all too much and something will come to her later. Hopefully, something shows up at Calvin's place to figure out who his supplier is." I say as Cody comes back in.

"Shop talk over?" he asks, pulling a fast food bag out of his jacket and setting it on the table beside my bed.

"I'll let you eat. Let us know when you break free of this place. You know the Chief has been calling this guy a few times a day for updates. Everyone wants to check on you," Rick says, pointing to Cody and then awkwardly shakes my hand.

Once Rick leaves, Cody takes the chair next to my bed. "I talked with Mom, and Skye really wants to come see you tomorrow after school. Mom wanted to know if you were in regular clothes, if everything would be hidden, and if it would be okay for Skye to come up," Cody asks.

I hate for Skye to see me like this, but fuck do I miss her.

"We can unhook the IV for up to an hour so she won't see all the tubes," my nurse says.

I'm not sure how I missed her walking in.

"Any chance you know when I'll be able to go home?" I ask.

"The surgeon will check on you tomorrow and sign off then. Your doctor has to sign off, too. It could be as soon as tomorrow night, but most likely, the next day."

"Let me think about it," I say to Cody because going two more days without seeing her is a bit too much.

"Okay, Mom will be calling soon, so you can ask her when you talk. Are you still okay with Calista staying with you and helping?"

Fuck, the thought of having Calista under my roof and in my space has given me some very inappropriate thoughts, especially with her brother sitting a few feet away. I haven't let myself think too much about it.

"Yeah, better someone I know and trust than some stranger," I say.

"You know there are plenty of people who would do it, all of whom we trust. She is just the most qualified, but if you aren't comfortable..."

I interrupt him. "I'd rather have her," I say rather too quickly.

Cody pauses and stares at me with a questioning look, but doesn't say anything. I don't want to let him know how much I like being around Calista. Growing up, Cody made it crystal clear that his sister was off limits to everyone. We even beat up a few kids who thought they could sneak around that rule and use Cody to get close to her.

Because of this, I never told Cody how I felt about her. My friendship with Cody means everything to me. So, I will do what I did then and lock the feelings up. I won't let my mind wander down the what ifs for too long. At least I will try.

"Okay, I think it's the best choice. I know I will worry less with her there to help you out," he says.

I cringe. Maybe he should worry more. I sure do. But it's just a few weeks, and I will keep the wall up. It won't be a big deal.

Just then, his phone goes off, and he checks it before turning to me. "Ready to video chat with Skye?"

"Yeah," I say, and he helps me sit up and put on a shirt to hide the bandages over my shoulder before he calls her and hands me the phone.

"Daddy!" Skye giggles and keeps glancing off screen.

"What are you doing, princess?" I ask.

She pushes some buttons on the screen, and the phone flips around, showing off a massive blanket fort in Cody's parents' living room.

"Uncle Colt and Uncle Kaiden helped build a fort! Want to see inside?" She's almost bouncing with excitement to show me.

"Of course I do. I think that's bigger than any fort we ever built as kids," I say.

"Oh, it is!" Colt calls from the background.

Skye giggles and walks inside the fort. The first thing I see is Calista in sweatpants and a shirt that molds to her curves, her hair in a messy bun. She sees Skye and smiles.

"Look, we are going to have a movie night in the fort!" she says. Then she turns the phone to show me the TV that has been put in the makeshift fort.

"Wow, I'm so jealous. That's better than any fort I've built," I say as the camera flips back to her face.

"Calista is going to braid my hair and paint my nails. After we have popcorn," Skye says, slipping back out of the fort and sitting on the couch that's been pushed out of the way. "When can I come see you?" Her voice is much more serious now.

I glance over at Cody, and he shrugs.

"Well, since it's the weekend tomorrow, maybe you can come and visit then," I say.

"Calista said she'd take me," Skye says.

"Mom wants to clean, and Dad needs to mow the yard," Cody whispers, letting me know why they won't bring her.

"Sounds like a plan. I can't wait to see you." Even though I'm trying to listen while she keeps talking, all I can think about is seeing Calista tomorrow.

"Calista is texting that they just pulled into the parking lot," Cody says.

I've been running this over in my head a million different ways, and my nerves are in full force as my nurse caps off my IV and turns off the monitors in my room. The goal is to make it a little less scary for Skye.

A few minutes later, she walks into the room, clinging to Calista's hand.

"Daddy!" Skye yells and takes off at a run, slipping from Calista's hand.

Thankfully, Cody catches Skye right before she launches herself onto the bed.

We spaced out my pain meds, so I'd be alert, but I'm definitely ready for my next dose.

"You have to be careful of Daddy's shoulder," Cody says, pointing to my shoulder, where my arm is in a sling.

"Does it hurt Daddy?" Skye asks.

"Yes, but it's healing and will soon be back to normal," I tell her.

When Cody gently sets Skye on my bed, she lies down and rests her head on my good shoulder, and I wrap my arm around her.

"Are you having fun with Calista?" "Yes. She does my hair every day," she says.

"How would you feel if she came and stayed with us for a bit after I got out of the hospital?" I ask.

"I'd like that. Why, though?" she asks.

"I'm going to need help, and Calista is a nurse. She will be able to help me until my shoulder and ankle heal."

"When are you coming home?"

"Hopefully, tomorrow. I am waiting on one more doctor to say it's okay."

Skye settles in and cuddles while Calista fills me in on some of the papers that have come home from school, and other things I should know about. Mentally, I make a note to add her to Skye's pickup list, at least while she is staying with me.

"Alright, I can't put it off any longer. I need to hook your IV back up," the nurse says, coming in a while later.

Cody picks up Skye, who watches everything the nurse does to hook my IV back up.

"I want to go home," Skye says once everything is hooked back up. Her voice is shaky and a little teary.

This is what I was worried about. I didn't want Skye to be scared or worried. I say goodbye, and Calista follows Skye, who is pulling her out of the room.

"We should have had her leave before the IV was hooked up," Cody says.

I just nod because all I can think about is how Skye went to Calista for comfort and how much they are bonding. It has to be because Calista is a female, and Skye doesn't have many women in her life. That must be the reason she is clinging to Calista. Right?

Chapter 12
CALISTA

Evan is coming home today. He got the okay early this morning. Mom had a doctor's appointment, so Cody is back in Whiskey River to pick up Skye, take her for a treat at the bakery, and keep her entertained until we get Evan settled at home.

That leaves me to go pick him up and get him home. To make it easier for Evan, I decided to bring my car. That way, he doesn't have to climb into Cody's truck. I have a bag that Dad packed of Evan's clothes and other items, so at least he'll be able to change into comfy clothes for the ride home. Yesterday when Cody finally left the hospital, he brought home the flowers and get-well cards, so I don't have to worry about them.

When I walk into his room with his bag in hand, it looks bare from the other day when I was here with Skye.

"I've got some clothes for you that should be easy to get into. I can help you get dressed, but I completely understand if you'd rather have your nurse help," I say.

He pauses and looks out the door and then back at me.

"My nurse said one girl quit last night, so they are short-staffed. I don't want to bother her."

"Okay, well, trial by fire, since this is what I'll be helping you with at home," I say. "Now, do you have anything on under the gown?"

"Yes, Don brought me boxers because I was not letting my ass hang out of the hospital gown," he cringes. "I'm sorry. I didn't mean to cuss in front of a lady," he says ruefully.

"I fucking cuss worse than Cody now. Don't hold back on my account," I say, smiling.

For a moment, his jaw drops, and he looks startled. Then, he grins at me.

"Of course, I don't cuss in front of Skye," I add.

"I appreciate that."

After I pull his pants from the duffle, it takes some maneuvering to get him to the side of the bed and then get them on. Already a little flustered, I've never been happier my dad grabbed a button-down shirt for Evan to wear. But when I look up with the shirt in my hand, my eyes widen. Evan has dropped the hospital gown, and his tan and toned abs are on display, along with a few tattoos on his chest and upper arms.

Damn, he's hot. But this isn't going to help me keep a wall up around him or ignore these weird feelings that are taking over at the thought of living with this man for a few weeks. It's obvious he feels slightly awkward as well.

"Listen, I'm a nurse. I help patients get dressed all the time," I tell him, trying to make him feel more comfortable, but it's also a reminder to myself.

Watching his muscles ripple as he moves to get dressed gives me thoughts I've never had for a patient before. Then I immediately try to shake the very inappropriate thoughts from my head of what I'd like to do to those abs and finish getting him dressed.

Then we wait because the nurse takes about an hour to come in with the discharge paperwork and instructions. There are pain meds for us to pick up, along with a bunch of papers to take home.

The nurse helps get Evan into a wheelchair and takes him to the front door while I go grab my car.

"Good thinking on skipping the truck," Evan says once the nurse and I have him all situated in my car and the rest of his stuff loaded in.

We swing by the pharmacy to grab his prescription, and then I make the drive to Whiskey River.

"Cody is getting me the paperwork today to get you added for pickup and drop off of Skye for school. I talked to them last week about getting you added and why, and they are working with me on it," he says as we leave Helena behind.

"Let me know what you need from me. I know most of the teachers there anyway," I smile at him.

Quite a few of the girls I went to school with who stayed in the area are teachers in Whiskey River now.

It's quiet for a while before he breaks the silence.

"I don't think I ever thanked you," he says.

"Thanked me for what?"

"For saving me that day. The Chief swears I'm alive because of you," he says.

I fight the emotions that are trying to push through and overwhelm me.

"You don't have to thank me for that. There was no way I'd have let you die that day or any time soon. Cody would kill me himself," I say, forcing a smile.

We make small talk the rest of the way home. He tells me about Skye's schedule and what she likes and doesn't.

Once we get to his house, it's just the two of us. Thankfully, his ankle is feeling better, and he can walk a short distance on it.

"Let's get you to bed," I tell him, wanting to get him settled soon so Cody can bring Skye home.

"No, I want to be on the couch. I know I need to rest, and I will, but I still want to be as involved as I can with Skye. She will have homework, and I want to hear about her day. But if it makes you happier, I will stay in bed all day until just before she gets home," he bargains.

"I can live with that as long as you don't overdo it," I tell him, then help him settle on the couch.

"You can take the bedroom across the hall from Skye. You will have to share a bathroom with her, but my bathroom has the better tub, and you are welcome to use it," he says.

I text Cody, telling him he can bring Skye home at any time. Then I take my bags up to the room he said I can use.

Once I'm settled in, I go to the kitchen to figure out what to make for dinner.

"Daddy! Daddy! Daddy!" Skye bursts through the door and runs over to Evan on the couch, but then stops in front of him and stares.

"You still have to be careful of my shoulder, but no more IV or wires, princess," he says.

After Skye visited Evan in the hospital, we had to sit down with her and explain what the IV was for and the different machines. She felt a bit better, but she didn't want to go back to the hospital even after she knew what they all did.

Hesitantly, Skye sits and makes sure not to jostle Evan. Then she begins a spirited recounting of her day and everything that happened as I say goodbye to Cody.

Finally, she models her hair, showing Evan what we did this morning. When Skye finally runs down, she grabs her backpack and starts working on her spelling homework. She sits at the coffee table letting her dad help where he can. Satisfied that they're both occupied, I work on dinner. At one point, Evan drifts off to sleep.

Skye finishes her homework and comes to me in the kitchen. "Daddy is sleeping," she whispers.

"Yeah, the pain medicine he is on will make him tired for a few days. Do you want to help me make a banana pudding for dessert?"

Her eyes widen, and she nods so fast that I think her head might fly right off her shoulders.

I set her up at the kitchen island to help me peel and cut banana slices with a butter knife. She then tells me all about her day, and I pretend I didn't hear it when she was telling her dad earlier.

Then we discuss how she wants her hair done tomorrow and what she wants for her lunch tomorrow and if it's possible to send her to school with banana pudding in her lunch. We decide no as that's a special at home treat, but I promise she can have some as an after school snack.

When I look, Evan is awake. He watches Skye and me giggle like we have a big secret as we look through hairstyles on my phone. There is an intense look on his face when his eyes meet mine. I offer him a smile before I turn my attention back to Skye.

When Skye realizes her dad is awake, she talks to him about our banana pudding debate and how she is ready for a big girl body wash like her friend.

Skye is definitely going to keep me on my toes over the next few weeks, but I don't think I will survive those stares from Evan.

Chapter 13

Evan

"Okay," Calista says to Skye after dinner and dessert. "I think it's time we get Daddy upstairs to his bed so we can get you ready. What do you say? Do you think you can help me?"

"Yes!" Skye says, taking it very seriously.

"Okay, you take Daddy's phone and make sure there is nothing on the floor between here and his bedroom. Daddy will move slowly, and I will help him up the stairs," Calista says.

"Will you turn on the heated blanket on my bed too, princess?" I ask Skye.

"You bet, Daddy!" Skye says, running off to do what she we asked.

"Alright, let's get you up, and once she is in bed, it will be time for another pain pill," Calista says.

I nod and let her help me stand up. My ankle is sore, but nothing like my shoulder if I move it too much.

Calista stands on my good side, helps me up off the couch, and waits for me to get my balance. She lets me lean on her on the way to the stairs, where I pause. Maybe I was overestimating my abilities right now.

"If you want to stay down here, I can set up the couch," Calista whispers.

"No, I can do this, but coming down to the couch might not be possible the next few days," I admit defeat.

"I didn't think so," she says softly.

Slowly, we work our way up the stairs. We get about four stairs up when Skye comes to the top of the stairs and I pause.

"Why don't you go pick out your PJs and clothes for school tomorrow and lay them on your bed?" Calista says.

"Okay!" Skye says, running off down the hall again.

"Thank you," I say and continue my slow assent up the stairs.

Just as we reach the top of the stairs, Skye finishes picking out her clothes and runs over to show me the outfits. It's the perfect moment for me to stop and catch my breath.

"Okay, now, why don't you go take a shower? I will be in to help wash your hair," she says, making Skye's eyes light up.

"She just plays in the shower," I say, while I slowly and laboriously make our way down the hall to my room.

"I know, but this gives her a sense of being a big girl. Then I'll go in to help with her hair and make sure she is scrubbed up and clean. I know it's not your routine, but I'm not here to replace you, so we made our own routines," she says.

I swear my heart is hammering like a train, and it has to be from the stress of climbing the stairs.

Right then, with her statement, the wall that has been firmly put in place crumbles. That she gets what it's like, just a little to be a parent, makes the task of ignoring her impossible. Suddenly, she is too close and is making me feel things I don't want to feel. Things that are dangerous to feel.

With that, I push myself to get to my room and into bed. I need some space. But before I know it, she is back to check on me.

"Alright, all settled in? Need anything?"

"Nope, I'm good," I say, breathing a sigh of relief when she leaves to check on Skye in the shower.

Day one, and I already feel like I'm losing my mind around here. It has to be the pain pills that are messing with me. Besides, she is Cody's older sister. She has zero interest in her younger brother's friend. I just need to not act on this over the next week or two, and things can return to normal.

The shower down the hall shuts off, and there are giggles coming from the bathroom. It's both Skye and Calista, and the sound goes straight into my heart. They are getting along so well, and Skye is happy. While I know she is happy with me, I've felt for some time that she has been wanting a woman around. How will she feel when Calista has to leave and go home? I already know I'm going to hate it, and it's only been a few hours for me, but Skye has been around Calista for several days now.

"Daddy! Will you read to me?" Skye comes running out of the bathroom, but stops at my door.

"Of course. Did you brush your teeth?" I ask her.

"Yes, and my hair, and I even put some of Calista's lotion on!" she says with a happy smile.

"Okay, go pick out a book."

When Calista comes out of the bathroom carrying Skye's dirty clothes and a wet towel, she looks at me with a question.

"Oh, the laundry room is by the back door behind the kitchen," I tell her.

"Ok, I'm going to run these down there," she says and leaves.

Skye is still picking out her book. Judging by how long it's taking her, I'm willing to bet she is pulling every book off her shelf to decide which one to have me read.

When she finally comes in with a book in her hand, Calista isn't far behind her.

"Calista, will you read to me, too? Daddy can do the prince's voice, and you can do the princess's voice," Skye says.

Waiting for my reaction, Calista looks up at me, so I smile and give my head a slight nod. I'm not going to deny Skye this despite my feelings. That is my problem, not my daughter's.

"Sounds good. Let's do it," Calista says, helping Skye onto the bed. Skye sits in the center near me, and I wrap an arm around her to hold her close. I missed her like crazy when I was stuck in the hospital.

Calista settles in on the other side of her, and my hand brushes against her hip, as she is leaning against the headboard. Neither of us moves. I don't know if she doesn't feel it or if she doesn't want to draw attention to it, but something about holding my daughter and having this small connection to Calista has me calm. I don't feel the pain in my shoulder, and there is this rightness that clouds everything.

Skye opens the book, and I start reading. Calista jumps right in at the princess's parts, and she gets really into the book with overexaggerated emotions. She even forces me to up my game while I'm reading. The whole time, Skye is giggling up a storm, and there is a huge smile on Calista's face, too.

"That was the bestest way I've heard the book read," Skye says when we are done.

"Okay, girlie, it's time for bed. Gently give your dad a hug and I will be in to tuck you in," Calista says.

Skye gives me a gentle hug and whispers in my ear, "I love you, Daddy. I'm so glad you are home."

I fight tearing up because she has no idea how close I came to not coming home again. That thought is what has been swirling around in my head for days.

"I love you too, princess," I tell her, trying to keep the emotion out of my voice.

Skye runs off to her room, and Calista turns to me.

"I'm going to get her settled, but then we need to change your bandage and get you settled for bed. Then I'll get you your meds because it's time and we need to stay ahead of the pain."

"Okay," is all I say. I have no intention of fighting her and making all this harder than it needs to be.

I listen as best I can as Calista gets Skye into bed for the night. She tucks her in and answers all Skye's questions, and as Calista steps into the hall, Skye calls after her.

"I really like having you here," Skye says, and her words squeeze my heart.

"Well, I really like being here. Now get to sleep," Calista says before turning off Skye's light and coming back to my room.

"Let's get you to the bathroom and brush your teeth, too."

Calista says this in a teasing voice that makes me smile and calms the concerns that are all piling up in my head.

She helps me out of bed and to the bathroom and, thankfully, leaves me to pee on my own. I'm able without too much difficulty to wash my hands and brush my teeth before she helps me back to bed. I'm grateful she isn't hovering over my every move, like I know her parents would be doing if they were taking care of me, which would be the case if she wasn't here.

"Okay, let's change this bandage and get it cleaned up. Then I'll get your medicine, and you can properly pass out for the night," she says with a smile.

Then she grabs a basket of supplies from my dresser that I hadn't noticed were there until now and helps me remove my shirt. There is a sharp intake of breath from her, and her eyes roam over my body like they did when she helped me get dressed earlier today. Taking a deep breath, she gently peels off the tape, holding my bandage in place. She doesn't take her eyes off the wound on my shoulder she is working on, but I can't take my eyes off of her. As she cleans the area around my stitches, she is gentle and careful. Finally, she pats it dry, rewraps the wound, and takes more care than my nurse at the hospital did.

Once she's done, she puts everything away.

"Alright, it looks like you are all set. What else do you need?" she asks.

"Well, that's a loaded question," I say before I get a chance to think about it and stop myself. "Sorry, I shouldn't have said that," I cringe.

"It's okay. I've heard worse from some of my other patients," she says with a small smile and seems to shrug it off.

"I'm not just another patient. I shouldn't have said it, and I'm sorry this whole situation is making me uncomfortable," I say honestly.

"I get it. But we are friends, I hope, and that's a good place to start. I can handle the jokes, and they make things more interesting, don't you think?"

Finally, I can relax. I didn't offend her, and I don't think I showed my hand in regards to what I'm feeling either.

"I think so. We will get into a good routine, and I promise not to make your job too hard either," I say taking the pain meds she hands me.

"Then I can promise not to cause you too much pain." She winks before turning and heading out of my room, closing the door behind her.

My dick is hard, and I haven't been this turned on in a long time.

I'm in so much trouble. And what's worse? I can't tell anyone about it, especially my best friend, her brother.

Chapter 14
CALISTA

While Skye is at school, Evan and I have fallen into a nice routine. If you can call it that, since it's only been one day. I got Skye ready for school, and my mom picked her up. We figured that for the first few days, until Evan was steadier on his feet, it would be best not to leave him alone. So, Mom agreed to take her with the promise that Dad would let her go home and take a nap since she had to be up so early. Dad happily agreed because it meant he could head out and have coffee with his friends and gossip about all the manly things like weather, hunting, and ranching. All the way around, it's a win-win.

After school, either Mom or Cody will pick her up and bring her home for the next few days. If someone is here with Evan, I will do it. At a time like this, it's really nice to have a big family to help out, and since Evan is considered family, everyone is happy to help.

While Evan is checking in at work, I clean up the kitchen where I made lunch. I'm lost in my own head when there is a knock on the door, and I about jump from my skin. If it was Mom or Cody with Skye, they would just walk right in, but she isn't even out of school yet, which I confirm by checking the time.

When I peek out the window beside the door, I spot Axel and Emelie on the porch. Opening the door with a welcoming smile, I see Emelie holding a large casserole dish.

"I hope it's okay. We stopped by because Phoenix and Jenna are watching little Noah, and we wanted to check in on Evan and see how he's doing," Emelie says as I step aside to let them in.

"How thoughtful of you! One meal I don't have to cook. Evan is awake, but let me go make sure he is up for visitors," I say.

"Okay," Emelie says. "I'm going to put this in the freezer. Cooking instructions are taped to the top, and it's disposable, so there's no need to worry about getting the dish back to me." Emelie smiles and walks toward the kitchen.

When I get upstairs, Evan is still on the phone. He holds up a finger, indicating he will just be a minute. The call quickly wraps up after that, and he turns to me.

"Axel and Emelie are here. Are you up for some visitors?"

"Yeah, will you clean off the couch so they can sit on it?" He nods toward the couch against the wall that has some clothes on it.

Picking up the clothes, I place them in his closet, close the door, and go downstairs.

"Come on up," I call to them when I get about halfway down the stairs.

Turning around, I lead them back to his room.

Axel is so large that he takes up most of the loveseat, so he pulls Emelie onto his lap, leaving me to stand or take a seat on the bed. I chose to sit at the foot of the bed so I could still see everyone, but I'm far enough away from Even that I can still concentrate.

"How are you feeling?" Axel asks Evan.

"Better now that I'm home. Still sore and tired. The pain meds help, but they kick my ass. I'm beyond grateful Calista is here because I wouldn't be able to manage Skye much less the house on my own," Evan says, sending me a look of gratitude.

"Well, we want to help any way we can. I put a chicken casserole in the freezer, and I'm sure the other guys will be by, and their girls will have food, too," Emelie says, smiling at me. "Do you think Cody can be here for a few hours later this week so you can get away and have coffee with the girls and me?"

"I will make sure he does," Evan says before I can answer. "She deserves a break, and since she is new in town, she needs to make some friends outside of Kaylee."

Evan adds that bit on about Kaylee because he knows I was about to mention I have friends because I have her. But I keep my mouth shut and smile. Even Kaylee says I need to make more friends.

"I'd like that," I say.

"Good, we are heading to the distillery later. I will set it up," Axel says like it's a done deal and already taken care of. I feel like I should protest that he's my brother and I should make the arrangements. Really, I could do it, but if they want to hang out with me that much and are willing to take care of setting it up and getting my brother to agree, I'm going to let them have at it.

"Why don't we let the guys chat, and you and I can go downstairs?" Emelie says, standing and taking my hand.

Before she can move, her husband grabs her other hand. She stops, leans in to kiss him and he finally lets her go.

I ended up having a great time with Emelie, just talking and drinking coffee. She helps me fold the towels and sheets I washed this morning until Axel comes down to collect her.

Before I know it, my mom shows up with Skye, who has a project for school to get started on.

Mom doesn't hang around. She has book club with some friends tonight, and Skye and I settle into the routine from last night of homework and getting dinner going while Evan naps. He wakes up for dinner and then helps Skye with homework as she talks his ear off before getting ready for bed.

Once again, she insists we both read her bedtime story. She picks a different princess book, and we read it to her. When she's finally settled and asleep, I help Evan get ready for bed.

"Your mom and dad offered to come over and help me out, too, you know. If you want to hang out with Kaylee or get out of the house there are people who can step in and help. You aren't trapped here all day and night. I want you to know that," he says.

"Don't worry about it because I'm not. This might shock you, but I like spending time with you and Skye. Basically, I am a homebody, so I never was someone to go out all the time. Just give me time to snuggle in and read a book, and I'm good to go," I smile at him.

"Well, it looked like you were going to turn down Emelie's offer for coffee, and I don't want you to say no because you think you have to be here all the time."

"I appreciate your concern, but I'm good with the way this is working."

When he flinches from the pain, I get out his pain meds and then help him up from bed and to the bathroom.

Once Evan is in bed, comfortable and halfway to sleep, I head to my room, change into my pajamas, and grab my book to read.

Getting lost in my book, I read a little longer than I had planned. When I look at the clock and see the time, I get ready for bed. Before I get a chance to turn off the light, a piercing scream comes from Skye's room. I jump out and run into the hall just as the light in Evan's room turns on.

"I got her, and I'll bring her to you," I call to him and rush into Skye's room to find her thrashing around in her bed.

Turning the light on, I carefully wake her up. "Skye, you are having a nightmare." I gently rub her back.

She wakes up and is disoriented, but she finally sits up.

"Here, let's go to your dad's room," I say, picking her up and carrying her down the hall.

Gently, I set her in Evan's bed, and she crawls to his side, resting her head on his good shoulder.

"Want to talk about it, princess?" he asks her, but then he looks up at me and mouths 'thank you.'

I turn to go back to my room when Skye calls out.

"No! Calista please stay!" she pleads.

I look at Evan since this is his room after all.

He nods to the other side of the bed.

"Okay, let me turn off all the lights in your room and mine, and I will be right back." I step out of the room for a moment to give them some space. Taking my time, I turn off all the lights and grab Skye's stuffie. There's no way she'll sleep without it.

When I get back to Evan's room, neither of them has moved, but both are wide awake. I hand Skye her stuffie, as she snuggled back into Evan's side. Turning off the light, I crawl into bed, keeping to the other side, but Skye reaches out for my hand. When I hold it, she brings it back to her side, pulling me closer to the two of them. My shoulder brushes Evan's arm, which is wrapped around Skye.

We lay there in silence, and before we know it, Skye is back asleep.

"She said the nightmare was of me getting hurt," he whispers.

"I am so sorry." I rest my other hand on his arm.

"It's my worst nightmare as a father. But I love my job too," he says.

"You don't have to make any choices right now. Just focus on getting better."

He nods, shifting to get comfortable. When he starts to drift off, Skye turns and lets go of my hand.

I use that opportunity to slip slowly out of bed and head to my room. It feels like I'm intruding on an intimate daddy-daughter moment, and being this close to Evan is doing funny things to my heart and my brain.

Chapter 15
Evan

I was looking forward to waking up with Calista in my bed, so when I woke before Skye and found her gone, I tried to push down the disappointment that kept creeping up. I shouldn't have even had her in bed with us. It was crossing a line, even if it was for Skye. The nightmare shook her, and I don't know how to make it better. It's a reality of my job and, thankfully, one I haven't had to face until now.

It's been on my mind all day, and today was one of the first days I didn't want to sleep all day, so there has been a lot of time to think about it. Calista is definitely more comfortable around Skye and me, and I can tell she is letting her guard down. The more she lets it down, the harder it is to keep my own walls up.

Does she know what she does to me? There is no way she's interested in her younger brother's best friend, but then I see how she looks at me and smiles at me, and my heart starts to hope.

"All right, let's get you ready too," Calista says, walking into my room.

Looking up, my jaw literally drops. She is wearing a tank top that hugs her curves and shows off her round tits that have been center stage in my dirty dreams ever since she has been back in town. She is also wearing cotton shorts, just long enough to cover her curvy ass, but I'd get a nice view if she would just bend over.

"Sorry, Skye was extra playful at bath time, and I got soaked so I just changed into my pajamas. I can go change," she says, blushing as she turns to go to her room.

"No..." I croak out. "It's fine, really. I just wasn't expecting it," I say, trying to recover from the shock.

"You sure?" She says, leaning against my doorway, wringing her hands and looking nervous, but cute as hell.

"Yeah, I'm sure." I'm more confident now.

I try to keep my eyes off her, but it's not easy. I find I'm leaning on her more than I was yesterday, and it's not because I want to be close. She doesn't say a word, but once we enter the bathroom, my eyes rake over her in the mirror, and when my eyes meet hers, we both pause, and neither of us says anything.

I'm not wearing a shirt because it's easier with where the bandage is. Several times, I caught her checking out my abs and tattoos. Before getting shot, I spent time almost every day at the small gym at the station working out.

At first, I thought it was all in my head, but watching her now, I don't think it was.

She isn't wearing a bra, and it's hard to miss that her nipples are hard and pebbled under her tank top. Fuck me, I realize that she's as turned on as I am. It's like something inside of me snaps. She seems to realize it at the same time because she clears her throat.

"I'm going to let you get ready for bed," she says, stepping out of the bathroom and closing the door behind her.

I guess she needs a moment to cool off like I do. Taking a few deep breaths, I prepare for bed. Even though I take my time, part of me wants to rush back there to her and see how far she will let me push things. Does she need space to think about what happened? Do I risk it all and see if there might be more between us? If I'm reading this all wrong, it could make the next few weeks awkward.

If she stays, and worst case, I scare her too much, and she leaves. She would then send Cody in to help, which will definitely make my recovery take longer after he beats the shit out of me.

After going back and forth in my head, I decide to let it play out and see what happens. I'm open to something more, but I don't want to make things weird with her either.

When I finally step out of the bathroom, Calista takes one look at me and jumps up from where she was leaning on the side of my bed. Her tits bounce and my eyes zero in on the bounty that is her breasts. Her nipples harden under my gaze, matching the way my cock hardens as I stare at her.

"I... umm," she stutters.

Her face is a sexy shade of pink, and it's really nice to know she isn't unaffected by this situation. The question is just how affected she is and if it's in my favor or if she can't wait to get out of my room.

"I need to change your bandage," she says after a deep breath.

When I nod, she comes to my side and lets me lean on her as I walk back to bed. Actually, I don't really need it as I've gotten up a few times myself to use the bathroom when she isn't here. But I'm not going to lose this opportunity to get close to her, to touch her curvy body. I love how soft her skin is, and her strawberry floral scent lingers even after she pulls away. Not to mention how my body enjoys it wherever she touches me.

Finally, with her aid, I get settled on the bed. When she walks over to the dresser to grab the basket she is keeping everything in, I get a great view of her magnificent ass. Her shorts have ridden up, and I can now see the bottom curve of her ass. Fuck, if I don't start leaking pre cum at the sight. Reaching for the blanket on my bed, I cover myself so I don't scare her off.

My body's reaction to her shouldn't be something she worries about while she's taking care of my shoulder. No matter how much I'd love for her to want to help me take care of other parts, too.

"I think the brace on my ankle needs to be redone, too," I say as she turns back around. I almost don't recognize my own voice.

"Okay, I will do that first, then," she whispers, setting the basket on the nightstand.

She is gentle as she removes the brace the hospital put on me. It's better than the ace bandage wraps I've used in the past for a sprained ankle.

"Here, let's stretch your ankle before I put it back on," she says without looking up at me. I'd kill to have her eyes on me while her hands are on me.

She puts me through some stretches that feel good and then she runs her thumbs down the muscles of my leg to my ankle before putting the brace back on.

"How does that feel?" she asks.

"Better than it should," I say without thinking.

Finally, she looks up at me, and I can see the desire and lust on her face. For a moment, I look surprised before I wipe it away.

Before I can even think about it, I decide to go for more. Pushing my luck, I order, "Put your eyes back on me."

When she looks up and meets my eyes, her cheeks turn pink. Otherwise, she doesn't react, but instead reaches for the basket before stepping closer to fix my bandages.

She starts by pulling out hand sanitizer that smells like lavender, and then finally, her hand is on me again. Stroking me. Then she gently pulls the bandage off. Is it my imagination that she is taking more time than normal?

Her eyes keep meeting mine, her nipples are still hard, and her breathing is rapid. Now I know this isn't in my head. I watch her every move and enjoy having her hands on me. Once she's done, I snag her hand and hold it.

"Thank you," I say, barely above a whisper.

"You don't have to thank me, Evan..." she says breathlessly.

"But I want to." I bring her hand to my mouth and kiss it gently, never taking my eyes off her so I can gage her reaction.

Her beautiful eyes light up, her face flushes, and she inhales sharply. I take that as a sign, so I flip her hand over and kiss the inside of her palm.

"Evan," she sighs my name like it's a prayer.

Gently, I tug her hand toward me. Not enough to move her, but enough to let her know what I want. I hold my breath waiting for her to make the choice. If she wants to turn around and walk out the door, I'd let her, and it would all end here. If she comes to me, then I know she wants this as badly as I do.

I can see the thoughts warring in her head because they are written all over her face. But I can see the moment she gives in and a moment later, she sits next to me on the edge of the bed facing me.

Dropping her hand, I use my good arm to reach up and cup her cheek, pulling her toward me. She comes willingly. I hesitate an inch from her lips, making very clear my intention and giving her time to pull away or change her mind. She shocks the hell out of me when she is the one to close the gap, and her lips land on mine.

But my surprise doesn't last long as I quickly take control of the kiss, wrapping my hand around the back of her head and angling her face so I can kiss her deeper. If this is the one time I get to kiss her, I'm not wasting the opportunity. I'm going to give it my all and make sure it's all she can think about for the days to come. Because this kiss is all I will think about for not only weeks and months, but years.

She moans and opens her mouth, allowing me to slide my tongue against hers. When she melts into me, it's my turn to groan because I want so much more than a kiss. My cock is throbbing, reminding me I've been ignoring it, and it wants inside of her. Then her hand runs through my hair, and I almost come at how good it feels.

That's when I pull back. I want more, but not here. Not like this when Skye could burst in waking up from another nightmare. That would not be something that I would ever want Skye to see. Ever.

"You know, I have been thinking about this a lot longer than I want to admit," I say, resting my forehead against hers, and we catch our breaths.

"That makes two of us," she says, shocking the hell out of me.

Chapter 16

CALISTA

After that kiss last night, I didn't get a wink of sleep. It was all I could think about, and for hours, I still felt his lips on mine. When my alarm goes off, I feel like I just closed my eyes. Even so, I'm up and getting Skye ready for school and making the coffee extra strong this morning.

When I take Skye into Evan's room to say good morning before my mom gets here, he is already up, and he doesn't look like he slept much either. With Skye at school and the house to ourselves all day, what will happen? I need a breather before I find out, so when my mom shows up, I'm excited to get away.

"Would you mind staying with Evan and letting me take Skye to school? I want to check on Kaylee while I'm out. I haven't heard from her in a few days."

"Of course! You need to get out of the house, too, and recharge. It will be good for Evan and me to catch up," Mom says.

"You okay with me taking you to school?" I ask Skye.

"Yes! I can show you where to drop me off!" Skye bounces out the door.

"Get in my car!" My mom calls after her, and she hands me her keys. "I have her car seat installed in my car, so it would be easier for you to take it instead of moving it to your car. Plus, my car is already warmed up."

I don't argue. Taking her keys, I give her a hug.

"Evan is already up, but he needs to eat and probably take a pain pill. He's been weaning himself off slowly, but he often wakes up sore and in pain, so he'll take one. Oh, and he'll try to tell you he doesn't need help getting out of bed, but he does. He's still a bit unsteady. I promise I won't be long," I say.

"Take as long as you need!" Mom calls after me as I put on my jacket and walk down the stairs.

It feels like I'm running away from Evan, leaving my mom at the house, so I'm not alone with him. But not only do I need to process that kiss, but I also I need to talk to Kaylee. Last night, I didn't want to wake her up, but I know I will catch her while she gets ready for work this morning.

Skye talks the entire way to school about what she'll be doing. Today is music class and she's excited.

How it's her turn to play the triangle, and how fun it looks. As we get closer to the school, she points out where to enter for a drop-off.

"Mrs. Fraser! This is Calista, Uncle Cody's sister. She's the one I told you about. She's staying with us and helps Daddy, and she has also been doing my hair. See the braid she did today?" Skye says to the teacher who opens the car door.

"It's very pretty. It's nice to put a face to the name she has told us all about this week. How is Detective Greer doing? We have all been praying for him," Mrs. Fraser says.

"He's doing better. He's still healing, but he's up on his feet a little more now that he's home," I tell her.

"Give him our love and let us know if you need anything!" She says before closing the door.

From the school, I go right to my apartment to chat with Kaylee. Thankfully, I can see the light on from the parking area, so I know she's awake, not that her sleeping would have stopped me from waking her up.

"Kaylee, I need emergency girl chat!" I say as I walk in. She peeks her head out of the bedroom and looks me over to make sure I'm physically fine. I follow her back to the bathroom.

"What is going on? Everything okay?" She asks as she keeps doing her makeup.

Putting the toilet seat down, I sit so I can comfortably share with Kaylee my news.

"Evan kissed me last night," I say.

Kaylee drops her eyeliner on the counter and spins to look at me. What?! Why didn't you call me?" She stares at me wide-eyed.

"I figured you were asleep."

"So, you wake me up! Best friend code says that is a legit reason to wake the other up! Oh my god! All the details now!" She demands, her makeup long forgotten.

I spend the next few minutes spilling all the details about the flirty comments, touches, looks, and kiss, ending with how I quickly bailed and left my mom there this morning.

"Oh, my god!" Kaylee squeals, but quickly sobers when she realizes I'm not gushing with her.

"Okay, what is it?" She asks, leaning against the bathroom counter.

"I'm so much older than him," I say.

"So, if he was older than you, it wouldn't even be a factor, so it shouldn't be now," she waves it off.

"He's Cody's best friend. My family is the only other family Skye knows. It would be so awkward if it didn't work out. I'd be the one to back away because otherwise he's lost his entire support group." I tell her everything that ran through my mind last night.

"Or you can look at it as you two already fit into each other's lives. You know each other better than most people when they start dating, and when this works out, it will be a seamless transition," Kaylee says, ever the optimist.

"And you think Cody is going to find out and say, 'oh cool' with a shrug and let it be?" I ask because we both know that is not how it's going to go down.

"I think he wants you both happy. While it will take some getting used to, he will be okay with it eventually when he sees how good you two are together."

"Everyone in town will judge me for being older than him."

"Fuck them. Again, if he were older, no one would blink an eye. Those who care about you two won't care at all. The rest don't matter," she says.

"Then there is Skye. She is already attached to me, and if it doesn't work out, she will be hurt, too."

"Kids are more resilient than you think. Plus, she won't lose you completely, the same way Evan won't lose your family. It will just be a different normal. Talk to your mom and dad if you need reassurance, but you should see where this goes. I saw the way that man looked at you. I wouldn't think twice if I could find someone to look at me that way," she says, finally picking her eyeliner back up and finishing her makeup. "The big question is, how did the kiss feel?"

I smile like a love-struck teenager.

"It was the best kiss I've ever had. He took control. But he was gentle, and the way my heart raced was like nothing I've ever felt before," I say honestly, making Kaylee sigh.

I think of that kiss again, and I can't stop smiling. It's been a long time since I've had something like this to be happy about.

"While I get that you are scared, but don't let the fear of striking out..." she starts saying the same line we have heard from my dad over and over again.

"... Keep you from playing the game," I finish and sigh because I know she's right.

"Alright, I need to go rescue my mom, and you need to get to work," I say, standing up and giving her a hug.

"Call me, no matter what time, next time something happens!" Kaylee says with a stern look.

"I promise to wake you up at two a.m. the next time Evan kisses me," I joke.

Laughing, she says, "That's all I ask!"

Chapter 17
Evan

It's been a few days since that life-changing kiss with Calista. There have been a few more stolen kisses and some heated glances but with Skye home for the weekend it was near impossible to find any time alone together.

I've made it down to the living room couch for the first time since I've been home, and those stairs took a lot out of me. But it feels amazing to be out of my room and have a change of scenery. Since Skye was back in school today, I was hoping to have some time to at least talk to Calista, but Rick came by this morning and only left when Cody stopped by.

Calista has been giving Cody and me some space, cleaning, and doing laundry. I hate that I can't help her. But one time when I offered to fold laundry while I sat here, she about bit my head off about resting and how it does not include laundry.

"Hey boys, I'm going to pick up Skye from school and get some groceries. Do you have any special requests, Evan? "

"You should request her blueberry French toast casserole," Cody nods my way.

"I've been told to request your blueberry French toast casserole," I say to her with a smirk.

"I'll grab what I need. You okay with bacon with it?" she asks.

"That's like asking if I want air with it," I chuckle, and she rolls her eyes.

"I'll be back in a bit," she says and gathers her things before heading out.

Once she is gone, I decide to talk to Cody and poke around a bit.

"She doesn't say much about her time in Chicago," I say, hoping to get him to open up and talk.

"Even though she wasn't a fan of the big city, she loved her job. She did a turn in the ER and another in surgery recovery, but when there was a management shift in the hospital, she got stuck with a boss who didn't appreciate nurses and couldn't keep his hands to himself. HR tried to sweep his behavior under the rug because of the spotlight having him brought to the hospital, and donors liked him," Cody says, finishing off his coffee and setting it on the coffee table.

"Is that why she came home?" I ask.

I know I've heard updates from her family, but I didn't pay much attention to her being so far away. It took all I had to learn how to be a single dad with a full-time job, and then Skye starting school. I feel like I'm just now catching my breath.

"No, she started doing in-home care, which led to her being recommended for hospice care. She did a few months there before it was too much, and she started talking about needing a change, so my brothers and I started trying to convince her to come home. It didn't take much persuading be-cause at that point, she was ready for a change. I'm glad she was here when you needed her. How is it working out having her here?"

I know I should be honest and tell him about the kiss and about my feelings, but this is my best friend, and he's made it perfectly clear since we were kids that his sister is off limits.

His family is the only family Skye knows, and I can't lose him if whatever this is with Calista should fall through. Skye would lose everything because of me, and that isn't fair to her.

If Skye weren't in the picture, I'd probably risk it all, but as it stands, I need to make sure there are more than a few stolen kisses with Calista before I talk to Cody.

"She has been a lifesaver. What made her choose Chicago after school?" I ask.

"She moved out there to take care of our grand-parents, Mom's parents. They needed help, but couldn't move to Montana and didn't want to move to assisted living just yet. They had a daytime nurse while Calista worked, and Calista was with them at night. A few years ago, Grandma was diagnosed with kidney failure, and she went fast. Grandpa had no desire to live without Grandma and went shortly after her," Cody says.

"Can you imagine being so much in love that you don't literally stick around long after the other goes?" I ask in awe, wondering if something like that is in the cards for me.

"I think it's possible. Just have to find the right one and not let fear stop you from taking a chance," Cody says with a far-off look.

"Sounds like you have a particular lady in mind," I say. Cody just shakes his head. "Nothing to talk about, but if that changes, I will let you know," he says.

"Not even a hint at who it is?" Now, I really want to know.

"She doesn't want anything to do with me, so it's not worth talking about," he says.

We talk some more about what is going on with the distillery and with his family before Skye comes running through the door.

"Daddy! Daddy! Daddy! I got a sleepover invitation!" Skye pushes a card in my face.

"She is so excited about it," Calista says, placing groceries on the counter.

"Need help carrying any more in?" Cody asks, standing up.

"Yeah, there are a few more bags, thanks," Calista smiles.

While Cody goes out to her car, Skye grabs my attention again. "Can I go, Daddy?"

I take the card and read it over.

It turns out Judy's niece is hosting the sleepover with her daughter. They are good people, and have watched Skye a few times when I was in a jam.

"Do you think you're ready for a sleepover?" You haven't spent time away from me other than at Nana's house," I say.

"I think so. They have games planned and movies, and we will be doing face masks," Skye says, excitedly.

Even though I want to let her go, I'm worried she isn't ready to be away from me for that long.

"She can always call, and I can pick her up if it's too much." Calista says as if reading my mind.

"I guess it would be okay so long as you finish your project before then and stay on your best behavior."

"I prom-ise Daddy!" Skye hugs me before running off to her room, hopefully to work on her project she is halfway through.

"That will be a perfect time to see if Emelie and the girls want to get together. I know Dad has been wanting some time with you, too," Calista says as Cody walks back in.

"Yeah, he has. I was supposed to talk to you about that while I was here," Cody says.

"Friday," Calista points her finger at him.

"Shoot Emelie a message and see if that works for her. It might take her a while to get back to you if she isn't in town," I tell her.

While Cody starts putting the food away, she pulls out her phone. Her phone dings before she can even put it down.

"I guess they are in town," Calista says, looking at her phone. "She says Friday at two p.m."

"Dad will be here," Cody says.

I smile at the fact that Calista is making friends with Axel's wife. He's become a good friend after he forgave me for bringing him in for questioning on possibly kidnapping his now wife. Her ex had filed false police reports. Due to a few other charges that were brought up, he served almost a year in jail for it all.

Now if I can just forget the fact that we will be all alone that night with Skye not here. It is the ideal time to spend some time together and see if this has the possibility of going anywhere.

Chapter 18

CALISTA

I roped Kaylee into coming with me to meet Emelie and the other girls. They seemed nice in the few short minutes I've known them, but you just never know. When you get people into a group like this, their personalities can change quickly.

With Dad hanging out with Evan, I don't even have the excuse to duck out early if it goes south. So I didn't give her a choice, especially since I knew she was off work today. My plans are to go to my apartment an hour before we were to meet the girls at the bakery, as I wanted to fill Kaylee in on the new developments.

"You know," Kaylee says, "with Skye at a sleepover tonight, I think it's the perfect time for you to figure out if this is going anywhere."

"I don't think so," I say. But in reality, my gut was telling me exactly what I should do: find out if there's magic between us.

"Think about it. No Skye busting in and disrupting anything or overhearing anything. This way you can figure out if this is something you two want to pursue. If not, then you can go back to normal when Skye gets home. If it is, then you go from there," she says, pulling her hair up in some fancy twist.

I hate to admit she makes sense because that means I have to act like an adult instead of burying my head in the sand and ignoring my problems, hoping they will go away.

"Well, for now, I can put that aside and worry about it later after meeting the girls. What do you know about them?" I ask.

"What little times I've run into them, they are super sweet. They mostly keep to themselves with their men on the mountain. But they have brought Jack and Evan into their circle, though the guys spend more time in town than the women. From what I can tell, loyalty means everything to them," she says. "Oh, before I forget to tell you, do not pass up the huckleberry bear claws at the bakery. They are extremely yummy."

I am a sucker for sweets, as my thicker thighs, and not-so-flat tummy can attest. So there isn't a chance in hell that I will be giving them up any time soon.

"Well, I guess we can't stall any longer," I look at the clock.

"Since all we have to do is walk across the street, I don't think we can," Kaylee smiles. Then, looping her arm in mine, she pulls me toward the door.

As we cross the street to the bakery, we take our time. My nerves are jangling and I'm nervous. This is why I turned down drinks with coworkers all the time back in Chicago. Getting a group of people together just isn't my idea of fun.

"Deep breath. I have an emergency plan in place if we need it, but I think we are going to have fun," Kaylee says.

Then she opens the door and we walk into the bakery.

Emelie waves to me from a large table in the back and then bounces over to greet us.

"Get some coffee, some snacks and come join us. A few of the girls are waiting in line." She waves at a woman who just paid for her order.

"I hope you don't mind. I brought my friend Kaylee with me. She was off work today, and I didn't want to leave her out."

A bright smile lights up her face and her eyes twinkle. "The more the better. We will save you two seats together," Emelie says, going back to the table, leaving us in line.

Kaylee and I don't say much as we place our orders to get coffee and a huckleberry bear claw before heading to the table where Emelie and the other girls are.

"I'm so excited you are here!" Emelie says. "I know there are quite a few faces, and we don't expect you to remember who everyone is. But I'm going to do a quick introduction. I'm Emelie, who you know. These wonderful women are Jenna, River, Sage, Hope, Jana, and Willow. Guys, this is Cody's sister, Calista and her friend, Kaylee." She points around the table as everyone greets us warmly. They seem really nice.

"First, how is Evan doing?" Hope asks.

"He's finally getting out of bed and spending time on the couch each day, so I can tell he's feeling better. His wound is healing nicely. From the looks of it, I don't think he will have much of a scar. He has a long road ahead with PT, though," I tell them honestly.

"Give him a gentle hug from me. He was one of the guys who helped me when my mom..." Hope trails off, choked up.

"When her mom kidnapped both of us," the woman next to her says, wrapping an arm around Hope. I think her name was Jana.

"He helped me with my uncle, too," Willow says.

I always knew Evan helped people with his job. Really, it was kind of in the job description, but to see that he's helped people right in front of me makes it hit home.

After that, the conversation flows with them getting to know Kaylee and me and letting us get to know them. Apparently, all their husbands are watching the kids down the road at Jack's shop. Even though the girls are having a good time, someone is constantly reading a text and sharing something funny that is going on down there.

Talking with them is easy, and I am included in many conversations. I'm smiling and laughing more than I thought I would. Before I know it, everyone is wrapping up their discussions and getting ready to head back to their families.

"We do this on a regular basis, and we'd love to have you both join us," Emelie says. "When I got here, there weren't many women on the mountain and I didn't have a lot of friends. As the guys started falling in love, I made more friends, and it meant the world to me. This is my family, same with many of the other girls. This is their family, too, since we don't have one outside of Whiskey River." Slightly teary, Emelie comes over to hug both me and Kaylee.

"I can't wait to join you guys again. This was lots of fun and I enjoyed meeting you all. I have to admit I was nervous about coming."

"Me too. I didn't even have to think about using my emergency escape plan," Kaylee says, making everyone laugh.

I walk with Kaylee back to my apartment, but I don't go up.

"I'm going to go home and let my dad leave before dinnertime," I say, but Kaylee sees right through me.

"You mean you want to kick your dad out so you can see where things go with Evan. Whatever happens, you better at least text me and let me know!" she says, hugging me.

"I will try." Then, getting into my car, I watch to make sure she makes it up the stairs into the apartment safely before pulling out of the parking lot and driving toward the mountain.

When I get to Evan's and walk in, I find my dad and Evan in the living room, talking and laughing while watching TV.

"How was your coffee meeting?" Dad asks as he stands up.

"It went a lot better than I expected. The girls are really fun, and I can't remember the last time I laughed so much," I say.

"He is due for his next round of pain meds in two hours if he needs it. Though he seems to be doing pretty good," Dad whispers in my ear.

"Evan, thanks for hanging out with me. I'll be back around later next week to get a few things done outside and get the garden ready for spring. Don't want you getting behind with such a short growing season," Dad says, shaking Evan's hand and then leaving.

"So, your get together went well?" Evan asks as I go into the kitchen to start dinner.

"Yeah, they are really nice, and they had such great things to say about you. Each one of them wanted me to give you a hug for them and tell you to rest up."

After pulling out the extra taco meat I put in the freezer earlier this week, I turn to him. "Taco salad sound okay for dinner? I know we just had tacos, but with it being just the two of us tonight..." I trail off to find Evan standing in the kitchen doorway.

"It sounds perfect. What can I do to help?"

"Nothing. Just rest. Don't overdo it," I tell him.

Nodding, he goes to a stool at the kitchen island to sit down.

While I make dinner, we chat about what the girls and I talked about and what he and my dad discussed. Scooping up the taco salad, I serve him and me, and then sit beside him at the kitchen island. All throughout dinner there are small accidental touches that I want to think mean something, but my brain says I'm overreacting. Like when his thigh brushes against me, or when his arm brushes mine. It just means we are sitting too close.

"Want to watch a movie after dinner?" he asks as we finish eating.

"Yes. Let me clean up. You go pick something to watch."

When we both stand, I go to move around him and grab the plates to take into the kitchen. But his hand on my hip stops me. He doesn't say anything until my eyes meet his.

"Thank you for dinner." He whispers as his thumb runs circles on my hip over my shirt.

After staring at each other for an endless minute, we both move and break the spell.

While I'm doing dishes and putting food away, I take a few extra minutes to calm my heart. I swear when he was looking at me, he looked right into my soul. He saw how much I wanted him and I was relieved at the look of longing which was written all over his face.

Once I can't stall anymore, I slowly make my way to the living room and find him sitting on one end of the couch with a blanket over his legs. When he sees me, he smiles and holds up the end of the blanket, inviting me to join him. Taking him up on his offer, I sit on the side with his good arm, so I don't knock or bump his injury.

"This movie, okay?" he asks. The movie he's asking me about is a romcom I used to watch almost on repeat when I was in high school.

"I can't believe you remember," I say.

"I remember a lot more than you might think," he says, starting the movie.

Chapter 19

EMELIE

"You have had a smile on your face since you got back from the bakery," Axel says once we are in the truck and heading home.

Our son, Noah, is in his car seat in the back and almost out. Something about the car and the diesel engine rumbling puts him to sleep almost instantly.

"I had a great time with the girls. Calista brought her friend Kaylee, and they both fit in so well."

"I'm glad, little one," he says, placing a hand on my thigh.

His one goal is to make me happy and he will move heaven and earth to make it happen. In return, I would do the same and I know these little meetings in town with his friends mean more than he would ever admit.

"I think Calista and Evan have something going on," I say. Though my husband appears shocked, he smiles at me.

"I'm not too surprised. Good for him. He deserves to be happy."

"I think so too, but he's her brother's best friend, and they have known each other since high school. Though I don't know if they will act on their feelings," I say, chewing on my lip.

"Whoa! I know that look. Stay out of it. I know you want to make friends and want them to be as happy as us. But we don't know these people as well as we know the rest of the men. We need to let it be."

"We can always get to know them." I say it with a smile and a puppy dog look on my face.

Over the years, I've slowly built this big family around us. After my ex broke up with me, I had no one. He was the only friend I had, and his parents were my foster parents and the closest thing to family I had.

Then I found Axel naked in the river, literally in the woods. I was lost and there was a storm rolling in. He took me to safety, and over the weeks, we feel in love.

When his friends met me, they were protective and welcomed me into their group. As the men fell in love, one by one, my friend group grew. I never thought I'd have the life I do now.

"Well, I'm just going to be there for her. I get the feeling she needs friends. Yes, she has Kaylee, but it's hard moving from a big city to here. Add in everything with Evan, and it's a lot. His cabin is fairly isolated and she might need more people around her. She didn't choose this life, not like I did," I say.

"You didn't choose it either at first. The storm locked you in with me. If it hadn't been for that, you have been right back to your old life," he says, angry at just the thought.

"Fate stepped in for us just like it will for Calista and Evan. I can feel it. They just need a little push," I say.

"More of a push than her living with him and taking care of him?" Axel smirks.

"Yes," I say firmly, because I can just feel it.

"Give it time, and let's see how things go once he's feeling better," Axel says.

"In the meantime, I think it's time one of the other women goes down and takes some food and checks in," I say.

We make the turn up the driveway, and neither of us says anything as we take the long, slow drive up.

As soon as Axel found out I was pregnant, he got the other men together and built the driveway so we could get the truck right up to the cabin. When I met Axel, we had to take the four-wheeler down to the gate where the truck sat. We did that for a few years. I had no problem with it and rather liked it.

Once I told Axel I was pregnant, it was one of the things he insisted on. He wanted everything to be as safe as possible for me and our little one.

Putting in the driveway was a long process. It had to be level in order to make it easy for the truck to get up and down. It involved some paving in certain places, and many trees had to be cut to make the driveway wide enough.

Then he insisted on building the addition to the cabin, so we had more space. Fortunately, the wood from the trees was used for the cabin add-on. Though I have to say, when my husband is determined to do something for his family, he gets it done.

Once inside, I head straight for the radio that the guys and us girls use to communicate since cell phone service isn't available this far up on the mountain. We all want to see Evan happy, so I know the girls will be on board in case we have to help it along.

Chapter 20
Evan

C alista is nestled close to my side, wrapped in a warm blanket as we settle in to watch a movie.

My brain is relentless in reminding me over and over again how her warm, cuddly body is snuggled up to me. I have no idea what is going on in the movie, only that the girl I had the biggest crush on growing up is burrowed against me. All I want to do is kiss her and never stop. But I also don't want to scare her off either.

Instead, to distract myself, I concentrate on memorizing this moment and enjoying the little things. Like her giggles at something that happens in the movie. Or the scent of her shampoo that surrounds me as she rests her head on my shoulder and the way the glow of the screen illuminates our faces and casts dancing shadows across the room.

Right then, her eyes meet mine and a smile lights up her face. Without hesitation, I lean in and press my lips to hers. They're soft and inviting and comfortable. It's like coming home after a long journey - everything falls into place and feels right again.

As our mouths meet, a jolt of electricity surges through my body, igniting every nerve ending. She melts into my body, and I crave more. I need her body close to mine, like I need a breath. There's too much space between us. So, I pull her into me, but before I can make my next move, she takes it a step further. Without any hesitation, she climbs into my lap, straddling it, while not once breaking the kiss.

I know she can feel how hard I am and how much I want her. Fortunately, that seems to spur her on. She grabs my hair with both hands, causing me to let out a deep groan. Suddenly, she stops, freezing in place.

"Shit, I'm sorry," she says, thinking she hurt me and she tries to pull away.

Stopping her, I wrap my good arm round her waist and pull her tight to me.

"That was a good groan, not a painful one. It feels so right having you near me like this." Then making my point, I lift up so my hard cock presses into her.

Her eyes widen as she feels me, but a shy smile crosses her face. She rocks her hips and the slide of her across my cock is heavenly torture. Tossing my head back on the couch, I enjoy every second of it. Keeping my eyes on Calista, her cheeks have a slight blush on them, and her nipples are diamond hard poking against her shirt.

"Maybe we should move this to the bedroom." I reach up and cup her breast, running my thumb over the hard peak through her shirt.

She pushes her chest into my hand and moans.

"Eyes on me, baby girl." I don't move until her eyes meet mine.

"Do you want this?" I need to know I'm not pushing her into something she isn't ready for.

"More than anything," she says.

"Then let's go up to my room. Our first time together isn't going to be a quickie on the couch like we are trying to sneak around before your dad and brothers get home." Smiling dreamily at me, she takes my hand as we climb the stairs. When we reach the top, she turns around.

"For the record, I wouldn't be trying to sneak around at my parents' house. There is someone always home and I would be way too scared of being caught," she says, flouncing into my room.

Growing up, once I realized I had a crush on her, I was scared to walk into that house and catch her with someone. So I always made sure I had Cody with me and he walked in the door first. Silly things my teenage self would imagine and the thoughts would run crazily through my mind. With one sentence, she put a younger version of me at ease. I wonder if she knew what she was doing with that one.

Once in my room, her nerves must be kicking in because she is suddenly shyer that she was downstairs. That's the last thing I want. Cupping her face in my hand, I rub my thumb along her cheek, grounding us both in this moment.

"You are in control here. You say stop and we stop. I want this but it's because I want you," I stress.

Right away, she relaxes and wraps her arms around my waist and pulls me in for a kiss. I let her take control of this one because I can tell she needs it. Though I do walk her backward toward the bed, letting the back of her knees hit the bed. Startled, she sits and looks questioningly at me.

It hits me then my arm is going to slow us down, but she's obviously waiting for me to make the next move. So I do.

"Remove your shirt," I tell her, not moving or taking my eyes off her.

I swear she moves in slow motion as each inch of skin underneath her shirt is revealed. My heart races and suddenly I want her naked to see all of her.

She is so much more beautiful than whatever I came up with in my head. She has curves that I can't wait to touch, and the blush on her cheeks is sexy as hell.

But she's looking down at her hands and nervously twisting them.

"What's running through that perfect head of yours?" I ask.

"It's nothing." She takes a deep breath, squares her shoulders, but won't meet my eyes.

"If it's bothering you, then it's something. Tell me, baby girl." I run my hand through her hair, wanting a small connection between us.

"It's just…" she pauses.

Giving her time to form her thoughts, I don't speak.

"It's just I'm older than you. I've got stretch marks, and my thighs prove I like cake over carrots…" she murmurs.

"I love your body," I say, reaching for her hand and placing it on my hard cock to prove my point. "Age doesn't matter to me. Your stretch marks make you human, and I honestly love your curves. Don't you dare start eating carrots over cake because I know that isn't you."

Reaching up, I unbutton my shirt, but she stops me, placing her hand over mine.

"Can I?" Her words are a mere sigh.

Unable to speak, I nod, watching her face as she slowly unbuttons my shirt. Even though she's seen me without a shirt every night as she helps with my shoulder, this feels different. Right now, her beautiful eyes are roaming over me like a whisper in the wind. When the shirt drops to the ground, her hand lightly traces over one of my tattoos. I want her with everything in me. And I don't want to wait another minute.

Catching her eye, I give her an order. "Take off your clothes and lie in the middle of the bed." I'm hardly able to get the words out just thinking of her naked in my bed.

If I was able to remove her clothes, I would take my time and kiss every inch of her skin, ending at her pussy. But with one arm, it makes that challenging. But I will make up for it as soon as I can use my arm again. Though there's no way I want to wait to have her and show her that I'm all in. All the way.

Watching her peel off every piece of clothing is the most erotic show I've ever seen. Her bra hits the ground, exposing her large breasts and hard dusty pink nipples. Then she slowly removes her pants and as they hit the floor, she steps out of them, standing in just her lacy underwear. I lose any sense of composure when they hit the ground and want to devour her.

Unhurriedly, she moves to the center of the bed and watches me as I just as slowly remove my pants and boxers. I reach into my nightstand, grab a condom, and toss it beside her on the bed before climbing between her legs.

I spread her wide for me and as I gently lean down to get my first taste of her, she tries to close her legs.

"You don't have to..." she trails off.

I pause for a moment. Who the hell made her feel like that? I don't want to think of her with other men because at this moment, I'm certain she won't be with anyone else ever again.

"Open your legs, baby girl. This isn't for you, this is for me." Without another word, I push her legs wide and kiss and nibble up the inside of her thighs.

When my lips connect with her clit, her back bows off the bed. She tastes sweet and I want more and more. With how vocal she is, I know she's enjoying this. I'm instantly addicted, and I'd spend all night down here if I could. But my cock is begging for attention, and the position is making my shoulder throb. I realize really quickly I'm going to have to put her in control, so I don't cause any setbacks.

Sitting up, I grab the condom, putting it on carefully with one hand, not once taking my eyes off of her.

"Scoot over," I say.

When she moves to the side of the bed, I lie down in her spot. "You are in control tonight. I'm pretty sure my nurse wouldn't be too happy if I hurt my shoulder any more than it already is," I say, smirking.

"Well, let's not upset her." Then, straddling my hips, she reaches between us to place my cock at her entrance.

"Eyes on me," I order. When I enter her for the first time, I want her eyes on mine.

Slowly she sinks onto me, and all I want to do is close my eyes and let them roll to the back of my head because she feels so damn good.

She leans forward to rest her hands on my shoulders, but stops herself and looks lost on where to balance herself.

"Grip the headboard, baby.

When she does as I instruct, the angle allows me to get even deeper.

With every thrust she is moaning, so vocal for me. It's such a fucking turn on.

"Slow down, baby, or I'm not going to last very long."

"We have all night." She gives me a wicked smile before picking up the pace.

Fuck, this woman is perfect. Reaching up, I wrap my hand behind her neck and pull her down for a kiss. I don't think I've ever been this turned on and I'm fighting to make it last. There's no way I want to get off before she does.

"Come for me, baby girl." I trail kisses down her face and neck.

Then, to encourage her along, I take one of her nipples into my mouth, sucking and biting it. Her pussy clamp down on me like a vise as she moans.

Kissing my way over to the other nipple, I nip at her again. Then I reach my hand between us and use my thumb to circle her clit.

"Evan!" She calls out, gripping the headboard tightly as her body starts to shake.

"Fuck, you are beautiful. I could look at you all day."

As she starts to come, her pussy clamps down on me even harder.

I'm trying to hold back my orgasm as much as I can so I can enjoy hers. But when she screams my name like I always imagined she would, I lose it. My orgasm hits me like a ton of bricks.

Calista collapses on me, resting her head on my good shoulder while we catch our breath.

After a minute, I gently roll her off of me and go to the bathroom to remove the condom and clean up. Grabbing a washcloth, I run it under some warm water and bring it back to the bedroom with me to wash her.

The satisfied hums, along with the cat eating the canary smile on her face, makes my heart thump harder in my chest. I did that. I satisfied her like that and it's a feeling I've never felt before.

Finally, I crawl into bed with her and pull her to my side. She puts the blankets over us and wraps her arm around my waist.

Neither of us speaks, but I can tell a lot is going through her mind just like it is mine.

"I'm not ready to talk to Cody about this." She tells me like she can read my mind.

My stomach turns at her words. I don't want to be her dirty secret because I am all in. But at the same time, it is her brother, and I have to respect how she wants to handle this.

"I'm ready whenever you are. I'm not going anywhere." I try to convey how I feel without scaring her off.

That seems to calm her because she relaxes and falls right asleep.

On the other hand, I'm sleepless with a million questions racing through my mind.

Chapter 21

CALISTA

I didn't get much sleep because as soon as one of us opened our eyes, we were waking up the other. Last night, I had more orgasms than I've had in my last few relationships combined.

Then, this morning, Evan woke me up with his head between my legs and was lazily eating me out. His words in my head from last night about how it wasn't for me, it was for him, make me so damn hot.

I've been with a few guys, and all of them saw going down on me as a chore, something they had to do to get me ready for what they wanted. But with Evan proving he honestly enjoys it? Fuck, this man is going to be the death of me.

I'm in the bathroom getting dressed, and every time I move, I'm deliciously sore. In my younger years, riding Evan the way I did last night would have been easy, but now it's a workout for sure.

When I pick up my phone before heading down-stairs, I see I have a missed call from Kaylee. I go outside to talk to her. There is so much to say.

"Calista?" she answers.

I just launch right into it. "Evan and I had sex, and it was amazing." She lets me go over all the details of how it happened, but once I'm into the story, I realize she was more excited by the kiss than this.

"Kaylee? What's wrong?" I ask.

"I know this is a big moment for you, and this is shit timing, but I'm finding it hard to be excited for you," she says.

My heart sinks. "What is going on?"

"I was brought in for more questioning by a not-so-nice guy at the station, who informed me that I am now a suspect."

"What the fuck?" I say before turning on my heel and marching my way back inside to confront Evan. He may not be working, but I know he's keeping up with the case.

"We will settle this once and for all," I tell her. As I go, I text Cody to get here and to sit with Evan. He asks if everything is okay. I say I don't know, but I need him here now. I'm walking inside when he informs me he's on his way.

When I walk into the room, Evan greets me with a happy grin. It disappears when I don't match it.

"Kaylee is a suspect. Are you kidding me?" I say, raising my voice.

His brows knit together, and I can clearly see the pain on his face.

"I can't talk about this. But she should go talk to Jack," he says, pleading with his eyes for me to drop this.

For a moment, I'm torn. Did he know she was brought in for questioning when we were sleeping together? I have so many questions, but this isn't the time for them.

"Have you talked to Jack?" I ask Kaylee.

"No," she says softly.

"Okay, listen. Cody is on his way to stay with Evan, and I'm on my way to you. I will go with you to see Jack."

"I'm scared." Her voice is trembling and all the fight is out of her.

"I know. Get ready, and I'll be there soon," I say, and we hang up.

"Did you know last night?" I ask the one question I have to know the answer to.

"No, I haven't talked to anyone at the station in a few days," he says.

As I move around the house to get my stuff together, Evan calls out.

"Don't, Evan. I will always choose her, and that is what I am doing right now. This is bullshit and you know it." I leave to go upstairs, to change my clothes and throw my hair up in a messy bun.

When I come back downstairs, Evan is standing at the bottom of the stairs.

"I'm not asking you to choose. Your fierce protectiveness of those who matter to you is one of the many things I love about you, and I'd never ask you to change. Tell Jack I told him to call Rick about the details, and he will get him everything he needs. I will call him when you leave, so he's ready," he says softly.

"Why do I suddenly feel like I'm sleeping with the enemy?" I look at my feet unable to meet his eyes.

"I want you to know I choose you. Whatever comes our way, I choose you," Evan says just as Cody bursts through the door.

I take a step back from Evan and don't say anything.

"What the fuck is going on?" Cody says.

"Kaylee is now a suspect in Calvin's drug case, and she is in full-on panic mode. I'm taking her to talk to Jack," I say, heading to the door and putting my jacket on.

When I look back, Evans's eyes are on me.

"I will be back later, and we will talk tonight," I say to him, and I can feel the relief in his eyes. A small smile and a nod is all I get.

"Go. I'll make the call," he says.

Getting in my car, I drive to Kaylee. Though I don't remember the drive to my apartment and before I know it, I'm parking and running up the steps.

"Kaylee!" I call when I walk through the door.

"I'm here and ready. Nothing I can do to hide the puffy eyes," she says, coming from the bathroom.

If I look hard, I can tell she's been crying. But only because I'm her best friend and know what to look for.

"I don't think anyone will be able to tell," I say, taking her hand as we walk out and down the street to the outdoor store Jack owns. Though I'm praying he is working today and if not, they can get a hold of him.

"Welcome in! Let me know if I can help you with anything," the girl at the counter smiles.

"Actually, is Jack in?" I ask.

"Right here," Jack says, coming from the back room.

"If it isn't that big city girl," Jack greets us.

I force a smile, and he picks up on it, his eyes going between Kaylee and me.

"Please tell me you are still taking on some cases as needed," I say.

"I am. Let's go back to my office." Then he beckons to us to follow him to the back of the store.

Once we're in his office, Kaylee and I sit on his leather sofa. After closing the door, he grabs a note-book and pen before he joins us on the leather chair beside us, instead of behind the desk.

"What's going on?" he asks.

"Evan sent us. As you have probably heard, he was shot at Kaylee's house when they did a drug raid after finding out her ex was selling drugs from her house," I start, and Kaylee joins in.

"While I was at work, I had no idea he was doing it. On the day of the raid, I came home early because I wasn't feeling good. I found Calvin in my living room. A few days before, I had broken up with him, so I was pissed he was in my house without an invitation. Then Evan was shot, and they put a pause on sweeping my house or whatever. I have been staying at Calista's because I can't go home," she says.

"Still?" Jack asks.

"Apparently. When I call, I can never get an answer about what is going on with my house. I was told they'd have some questions, which I figured they would. Well, I was called in yesterday and told I'm a suspect. They tried to ask me a bunch of questions. I don't know much, but I've watched enough shows to tell them I wasn't answering any of them. They didn't hold me, so I guess that's good."

"Evan won't talk about it, but he told me to have you call Rick at the station for the details," I add.

"Okay, so if they call you in, you have them call me. You did the right thing by not answering any questions. You don't speak to them unless I'm there.

It's your right to have a lawyer present at all times," Jack says.

After Jack has both of us give him all the details we can from the raid and the day Evan was shot, he goes to his desk and makes the call to Rick.

Nervously, I turn my phone over and over in my hands. While I want to text Evan because last night was mind blowing, I also feel like doing so will break some kind of friend code. Right now, she really needs me.

Jack has a commanding presence on the phone and a calming one when talking to us. It's the first time I've had a chance to relax, and my brain is racing. Evan is on one side, and Kaylee is on the other, but I don't see a way to bridge that gap right now. I really hope Jack has better luck.

Chapter 22
Evan

Watching Calista walk out the door, it feels like my heart is going with her. Hopefully, I can make this right because I'd never ask her to pick me over her best friend. At the same time, I'm not ready to walk away from my job either. But I have always believed in doing what is right, and unless they uncovered something big they are keeping from me, it's not right to list Kaylee as a suspect.

"What the fuck is going on?" Cody asks as he helps me get back to the couch, not that I need his help.

"Let me call Rick first, then we can talk," I say, pulling out my phone.

"I was waiting for your call," Rick answers.

"What the fuck is going on?" I echo Cody's question. "You really think Kaylee is a suspect?"

Cody's head snaps up at that and looks at me. I can see the questions on his face, but he keeps quiet.

"Listen, I don't know what to think. My gut says no, but Calvin flipped on her. He told us where in her house to find the drugs, and when we looked, they were there. Also, he says she knew and was even getting a cut of the money," Rick says.

"Did you subpoena her bank account?" I ask.

"Yes, no unexplained deposits. She still owes on her car, credit cards, plus she has a student loan. Normally, that's the stuff that gets paid off when they get money. It's doesn't add up, and we didn't find any extra cash at her place either," Rick says.

"You don't think Calvin planted that stuff for exactly this moment?" I ask.

"I don't think he's smart enough, but I think whoever he is working for told him to do it and they had this plan in place before he was ever caught," Rick says.

"We just can't prove it," I sigh. "Why didn't the drug-sniffing dogs find the drugs when they were in the house?"

"They were placed in a frozen TV dinner box at the back of the freezer with meat stacked on top of it."

"He had drugs stored in the freezer?"

"Yeah, that's a new one for me, too. They brought her in for questioning and she wouldn't answer anything. Didn't ask for a lawyer, but just kept saying she knows better than to answer that question," he says, making me smile.

She is smart, and that right there might have saved her ass.

"Listen, there are a lot of coincidences in this case. They conveniently broke up days before the raid, and all this happened while she was at work. But that day, she was at home. Then you're wounded, and her story of not feeling good is forgotten as she was at Calista's side all day," he says.

"Well, she is meeting with Jack now. He's going to call you for the details and also going to ream your asses for keeping her out of the house this long. This isn't a murder case. Anything past two days is excessive, and that could botch this whole thing. With how long you've kept her from her house, and then drugs show up, can you prove they weren't planted?" I say.

"Fuck, whose side are you on?" Rick grumbles. "Most everyone headed to the hospital when you were shot, and we have been buried under paperwork and petty crime call-ins, and we are down. Another guy's mom died across the country and is on leave."

"I don't know what is going on there, but the department is fucking this one up and is about to look really bad. Get your shit together and stop letting those young bucks walk all over you," I say, hanging up.

Leaning my head back on the couch, I close my eyes.

"Calvin is trying to say Kaylee knew about the drugs and was even getting a cut of the money. They are still holding her place as a crime scene, which is not normal under the circumstances. Then, convenient- ly they found drugs where Calvin said they would be. But on the day this happened, we had dogs in there to clear it, so it's not adding up. I don't have a good feeling. I'm on leave, but still being kept in the loop on the case. Honestly, something is off, I can feel it in my gut."

I won't admit it out loud, but I wonder if someone at the station is involved with Calvin. Though I have no way to prove it right now. Nor will I throw any of my guys under the bus without a load of proof. Yet my gut is screaming and I've always trusted it.

The argument I heard before we burst in was full of pain and anger, not the kind someone can fake. Plus, let's be honest. I've seen Kaylee's acting skills, and she is horrible and stiff. You can tell she is reciting lines. My gut says she is innocent. Her best friend was in panic mode because of me, so of course, she pushed through not feeling good.

"When you brought in Kaylee after I was shot, how was she feeling?" I ask Cody.

He stops to think before he answers.

"She was pale, and wanted nothing to eat. She stayed in the waiting room with us and fell asleep with her head on Calista's lap at one point while we waited to hear about you. When she woke up, her color was back and she ate a bit. Whatever it was, she needed to sleep it off," he says.

"Was there anyone from the station there?" I ask.

"No, they had asked Calista to update them. Rick showed up right before we were able to see you, but Kaylee was awake by then. Why?"

"I'm just trying to think of everything they are using against her. Would you testify to that if needed?" I ask.

"For Kaylee? Hell yeah, I would. How bad is this?" Cody asks.

I don't miss how protective he is of Kaylee and I wonder if it's because she is his sister's best friend or if it's more.

"I shouldn't say anything, but something isn't adding up, and I think Kaylee is being set up to take the fall."

Cody's face fills with anger, but I keep talking before he can go off.

"Calista was heading to take her to Jack with instructions to call Rick. If anyone can get to the bottom of this, it's Jack. She is in good hands, especially since I can only do so much without getting in trouble at work," I sigh.

"Spill it," Cody says, knowing me well enough to know there was more behind that sigh.

"Skye has been having nightmares about me getting hurt. It was always there, the risk with my job. But now, I'm facing it head-on and need to make a decision. I don't want her scared every time I go to work. I love my job, but I'm not sure that I want to continue making my daughter worry that I'm not coming home. There's also the fact, I don't want to put my life on the line again. We are too short-staffed to try to get a desk-only job, so that leaves me with a choice that has been running through my head since I've been home," I tell him honestly.

"Well, you have time to work it out because you won't be back on the streets anytime soon. Don't make a rushed decision, and you know we will support you whatever you decide," he says.

I believe him. The problem is I have more than just Skye to consider now. I want to take Calista into account, but I can't tell him that. There is this part of my life I can't talk to my best friend about just yet, and it's killing me.

"So, distract me. What is going on at the distillery?"

Chapter 23
CALISTA

O nce I got home, Evan and I were able to have a short talk. But with Skye around, it was difficult to keep it from her or get into a lengthy discussion. We had to wait until she was in bed.

Evan made it very clear he wasn't going anywhere. I made it clear that I couldn't fully commit until I knew everything was going to be okay with Kaylee. He said he was fine with that. Then we had the hottest quickie before I snuck back into my room for the night.

Today, Evan, Skye, and I are heading downtown to the BBQ event to support the distillery. Not only is this the first time Evan will be out in town, but it's also one of the first years he won't be participating in the BBQ festival.

Thankfully, his friend Rick was willing to step in for Evan at the festival, so the police charity will still be up and running. Though I know Evan feels bad about it and always enjoyed participating.

"I can't wait to try Uncle Cody's barbecue sauce. But I bet it's not as good as Daddy's," Skye says from the backseat.

At her words, I look over at Evan, who is in the passenger seat, to see what his reaction is.

"Uncle Cody told me he will have some really spicy ones, but promised to have a mild one just for you to try," Evan says.

"I can handle spice, Dad!" Skye says.

"Not this kind of spice. It's the kind that will burn your tongue and make you cry," I say with a smile.

Giggling, Skye asks "Why would he do that?"

"I don't know. You will have to ask him when you see him." I'm just as interested in his response as Skye is now.

When we get downtown, the festival is already in full swing. Fortunately, Cody gave us a pass to put on our dashboard to park in the employee parking of the distillery. Taking the back way in, we use the directions he gave me to find the parking area. The area is blocked with a cone, so I get out to move it and put it back when I'm done. It's a very small price to pay for a premier parking spot.

"Let's go into the distillery and say hi to my brothers before we check out the rest of the festival?" I say, almost like a question.

"That works for me," Evan says.

I get out of the car and walk over to his side to offer a hand, but now that his ankle is feeling better his shoulder is the only obstacle. It doesn't really stop him from getting in and out of the car.

"It should be me coming around to help you out of the car," he says with a pointed look as I reach for the back seat door to help Skye out.

"Well, I look forward to it once you are able to drive again. Until then, you get to let me pamper you," I say, smiling. When we walk into the distillery, there is no stopping Skye as soon as she sees Cody.

"Uncle Cody!" She yells and runs right to him, not caring that he's talking to the couple in front of him.

Cody doesn't miss a beat. Smiling at her, he bends down to pick her up, settling her on his hip while he finishes talking to the couple. Skye waits, resting her head on his shoulder while he talks.

Moments like these are what I miss, and I hope one day Cody will get to be the uncle to my kids just like this. Maybe one day. They are so cute together that I pull out my phone and snap a few photos.

"Will you send those to me? That one would be framed on the mantle," Evan says in my ear.

Just being near Evan has me on alert, but his whisper in my ear sends shivers down my spine. Trying not to show how aware of him I am, I quickly send the pictures off to him. ،

Once Cody is done talking to the couple, he comes over and joins us.

"Hey, princess. Excited for the festival?" Cody asks.

"We just got here," Skye says.

Turning my phone, I show Cody the photo I snapped of him and Skye. That picture captures Cody's smile and the love in his eyes as he holds Skye.

"Will you send me a copy of it?" he asks.

"Already done," I smile. I figured he'd wanted one, so I sent it to him when I sent it to Evan.

"Come on, let's do a bit of tasting," Cody says, turning to go to the counter.

"Oh, can we taste the sauce?" Skye asks.

I start to giggle because in this place that could mean so many things.

Thankfully, Cody knows exactly what she means and heads right to the barbeque sauce tasting area before setting her on the counter.

"Okay, I made this one, especially with you in mind." Cody puts some sauce on a cracker and hands it to her. Then he makes one for Evan and me.

Taking a bite, the sauce is mild and flavorful. Kind of like the sauce he's always making at home. You can taste a bit of the whiskey flavor around the barbeque tang.

"I like it!" Skye gives Cody a thumbs up. "I want to try that one," she says, pointing toward the spicy one with a flame on it.

"That one is really spicy. Like burn your mouth, make you cry spicy. I don't think it's for little princesses," Cody says with a wink.

"Please, Uncle Cody?" Skye turns on the puppy dog eyes, and Cody looks at us for help.

"She has to learn someday," Evan says, cringing.

"Let me get a carton of milk ready." Cody reaches under the counter to where I'm sure he has a mini fridge.

"What's the milk for?" Skye asks.

"Well, when something is too spicy, you drink milk and it helps relieve the burn," Cody says.

He then gets the spicy barbeque sauce on a cracker for Skye. Thankfully, he puts less than half the amount he placed on the mild one.

She confidently takes a bite and starts chewing. I'm filming the whole thing, and you can see the moment the spice hits her. Her smile drops and her whole-body freezes and she even stops chewing. Her little eyes water and Cody does well keeping a straight face while taking the rest of the cracker from her and handing her the milk. She chugs it faster than I've seen her eat or drink anything before.

I'm trying to hold back my laughter and keep the phone and video steady.

"It's so spicy," Skye hisses out once she drinks all the milk.

Evan, Cody and I all lose it.

Turning the video off, I lean on Evan I'm laughing so hard. When I finally catch my breath again, I look up and Cody is looking at Evan and me with an odd look on his face. Shit, did we slip up? All I did was laugh. If Cody had been beside me, I'd have been leaning on him. Cody turns back to Skye and the look on his face is gone.

"So will you take my word for it next time, princess?" Cody asks.

Skye nods solemnly. "Not the spicy one, ever."

We all chuckle at the look on her face.

"You guys want to try some of the whiskey?" Cody asks.

"I can't, I'm driving, and Evan really shouldn't with the meds he's on," I say.

"Let's go grab some food. We can try a little sample later. It can't hurt," Evan says.

Taking Skye's hand, I turn toward the door. Looking back, I lock my eyes with Cody and he just laughs.

We follow Evan out the door into the crowd. We walk up and down Main Street, stopping and talking to people, and tasting food at different booths for a couple of hours. After a while, I can tell Evan's shoulder is bothering him.

"I'm getting pretty tired. Why don't we make our way back to the distillery?" I say.

I know I was right because he seems relieved and ready to go back.

"Just a little more time?" Skye pleads.

"I think your dad needs a little rest, too. Let's go see what Uncle Cody is up to," I say.

She darts a look at her dad, and then she doesn't protest any more.

When we get back to the distillery, Evan takes Cody up on the whiskey sample. He's a grown adult and while I don't think it's a good idea, I also can't stop him. Since I'm driving, I turn down the drink. Cody thought of Skye and he has apple cider that they just got in for her to try.

Once all the samples have been drunk, we go back to my car and head home. Skye falls asleep on the way home since it's about her bedtime. When we get to the cabin, she doesn't even wake up.

"I hate to wake her up for a shower," I say, looking at how peaceful she is.

"Don't wake her. Just take her to bed. She can shower in the morning," he says with a goofy smile on his face.

Shaking my head at his silly smile, I get out of the car. He opens the door for me while I carry Skye inside. I'm shocked that I get her to bed and remove her jacket and shoes all without her even stirring.

"She's a deep sleeper that one," I joke with Evan when I walk into his room after putting Skye to bed.

He closes the door behind me, kissing me pressed against the door.

"I was doing a lot of thinking today," he says between kisses.

"Oh yeah? About what?" I am unable to stop smiling at how playful he's being tonight.

"You should move in with me." He kisses down my jaw, oblivious to how I freeze at his words.

Cupping his head in both hands, I hold his face in front of mine, studying it.

"You're tipsy," I sigh, knowing the little alcohol he had more than likely mixed with his meds has hit him harder than he realizes.

"Am not. Either way I wouldn't say it if I didn't mean it," he says, kissing my neck. "Stay with me tonight."

I shouldn't, but I agree because I miss sleeping in bed beside him. Even if it was only the one night.

He leads me to bed and pulls me down to snuggle with him.

"I had the biggest crush on you when I was in school," he admits, staring up at the ceiling.

"Really?" I ask. I thought maybe he did, but I didn't know for sure.

"Yeah, but you were older. Cody made it clear, as did all your brothers, that you were off limits."

"Plus, I was way too old for you. I still am," I say.

"Doesn't feel like it when you are lying here with me like this," he says.

Dammit, he's right because it doesn't. It feels right.

"I think the age thing is your way of keeping a wall up, even if it's a flimsy one," he murmurs, turning his head to kiss my temple.

"Maybe, but do you want to talk about it or take advantage of the fact that your daughter is passed out for the night? Should I lock the door or go back to my room?"

"If you try to go to your room, I'm just going to follow you. Your choice," Evan says.

Smiling seductively, I stand up and walk over to the door. His eyes stay locked on me, daring me to leave. It's so sexy. That look makes me want to jump him. And why not? So, I slowly close the door, lock it, and then rip off my shirt.

"Good choice, baby girl," Evan says.

It feels like the right choice for now. Hopefully, I'll feel that way in the morning.

Chapter 24

Evan

Today Calista is taking Skye to school and I've been deemed capable of staying on my own for no more than an hour at a time. I'm rolling my eyes at the thought. It was a talk with not just me and Calista but Skye, Cody, and his parents.

Even though I feel ready, I am slightly nervous being on my own this morning. After I get dressed, I go downstairs, hoping Skye comes home with another sleepover invitation. Or maybe I can find a way to convince Cody's parents to take her for a night without raising any questions. What I really want is another night of Calista in my bed, but she won't stay there when Skye is in the house.

As soon as Calista walks through the door, I pull her into me and kiss her.

"I really hate waking up without you in my bed," I tell her.

"You can't be used to it. After all, it only happened twice," she says, smiling big.

"Yet I'm already addicted." I take advantage of the moment and kiss her neck, while pulling her all the way into the house.

"We need to talk," she says, taking my hand and leading me to the couch.

My body gets cold. In my experience, when a woman says we need to talk, it's normally not a good thing, and I'm not going to like the outcome. Sitting, I pull her near me. I already know I'm going to fight for us, and having her close will help.

Once we're settled, she pauses. Then she's biting her lip and looking anxious, so I take her hand in mine and rub my thumb over her knuckles.

"You can talk to me about anything," I say gently.

"The night of the BBQ Festival, do you remember what you asked me that night?"

All I want to do is grab her and then kiss her in sheer relief. Instead, I keep a straight face to see if she is going where I hope she is.

"I asked you to move in with me," I tell her confident-ly.

There is a sharp intake of air from her, but she doesn't say anything.

"You thought I had too much to drink, but I meant every word."

"Evan..." She starts.

"Listen. I have thought this out. I really like having you here, but our time here is limited. If you stay here, I know it means talking to your brother. But I want you to be mine, and I want everyone to know." I lay my cards on the table and watch her reaction.

Her eyes go wide, and I swear I see something like fear on her face. Fuck, maybe she isn't ready for such a big commitment, and there is a good chance I've scared her off.

"We can move at whatever pace you want. We don't have to tell Cody right now. But, baby, I'm not going anywhere." I squeeze her hand.

My words seem to be enough to calm her for right now. Though I hate the idea of continuing to hide our relationship from my best friend. But if that is what she needs, I will give it to her. At some point, we are going to have to talk about it. There's a reason she is holding off letting her brother and family know about us.

"I don't want Cody to know about us yet," she whispers while looking down at our joined hands on her lap.

"If that is what you want, then so be it. But can I ask why?"

She looks up at me, and I can see the hesitation on her expressive face. Right now, she isn't ready to talk about it. But I'm stubborn and I want to know, so I wait it out. She's going to have to give me something, anything.

"Because he will ruin it," she says, tears welling up in her eyes.

Deciding not to push it, I pull her into my lap, wrapping my arm around her.

"I can't be the reason you lose your whole support system. Cody, my parents, and my brothers are all Skye knows. I don't have a great track record with relationships, and there is more to think about than just me with this one," she says.

I know she means Skye.

"I'd never do anything to hurt my daughter, but Skye loves you. Even if things didn't work out with us, I know you would still be in her life," I say.

"I'm only here for another week or two. Until then, I think we need to get this out of our system. When I go home, this has to end," she says, tears welling up in her eyes.

The emotion in her voice tells me that it isn't exactly what she wants.

My heart breaks. The last thing I want to do is give her up and end this. But my heart is convinced we can make this work. When she's ready to leave, I'm sure that I can persuade her to stay and make a life with me and Skye.

"If that's what you want, then we will keep sneaking around," I say.

She looks sad, and the thought of her being anything but happy kills me. But right now, she doesn't know she's mine, and this isn't ending in a week or two. But if that is what she has to tell herself, then so be it.

I pull her in for a kiss.

She thinks she is walking away in two weeks. But I plan to make it impossible for her to do so.

Then, putting all that aside, I kiss her until she melts into me. My dick is hard and all I want to do is strip her of her clothes, feel her luscious body against me and make love right here on the couch.

At least, that is the plan until someone knocks on the door.

"You expecting anyone?" She tries to pull away from me.

"No. Are you?" I ask, already knowing she isn't.

"No."

I bought this cabin in the mountains because there are no neighbors, and it isn't the kind of place someone will just swing by.

"Stay here," I tell her. Getting up, I grab the gun I keep locked up on the top shelf of the coat closet.

"Evan!" she hisses.

Ignoring her, I open the door, holding the gun in plain sight.

"Mind not pointing that at my wife?" Cash growls.

When I realize Cash and his wife, Hope are standing there with a casserole dish in her hands, I set down the gun.

"We wanted to swing by and check in on you, and bring some food to give Calista a break on cooking one night," Hope says.

I let them in and Calista gives me a look.

"I can't believe you opened the door with a gun," Calista huffs, giving Hope a hug.

"Oh, it's normal with the men out here," Hope says. "They move to the mountains because they don't want unexpected guests. Bennett has greeted me with a shotgun in my face. Every time I visit Jana, Cole opens the door with a gun, even when he knows I'm coming," Hope says like it's nothing. They both head to the kitchen to put the casserole away.

"I've talked to Cole many times about that one," Cash grumbles.

"I don't think you will ever get him to break that habit. Not when the whole reason he met his wife is because someone kidnapped her," I say.

Cash sighs, but there is a hint of a grin there.

Both Hope and Jana were kidnapped by Hope's mother. Cole was one of the men who raided the cabin before I could get the other cops there. I didn't approve of how he handled it. Now, I know if it had been Calista in there, I wouldn't have followed protocol either. Also, I know without a shred of doubt that Cash and the other guys would have been right on my side.

When Cole walked in and saw Jana there, that was it. He's been obsessed ever since. Wouldn't leave her side, and the two of them are happily in love.

"You up for some company? Hope has been talking my ear off about spending more time with Calista since the girls met up at the bakery," Cash says.

It appears that the girls have settled in the kitchen talking and Calista already has a large smile on her face. Right now, she looks at home and I want her to know there is more to a life with me then just sex. She can have a life here.

"Yeah, some company would be great," I say, as we sit on the couch.

When I bought it, I wanted to fill this house with family and friends. Suddenly it hits me it might not have been the conventional way of doing things, but that is exactly what's happening. And I'm more than happy with it.

Chapter 25

Calista

The last two weeks have sped by faster than I wanted them to. During the day, Evan had a few doctor appointments, which cut into our alone time. He's been cleared by his doctor and is starting physical therapy. After proving he could manage around the house, I ran out of excuses to stay. Today Cody made a big deal about helping me move back to my own place.

Sneaking around at night once Skye is in bed seemed easy at first, but it started to wear on us both. He asked me every night to stay in bed with him, but I insisted on going back to my room. Last night, he followed me. He said if it's our last night together, he was going to spend every minute with me. In short, neither of us got much sleep.

I don't want to go, but he hasn't asked me to stay. Now, with everything in me, I want him to ask me again. This last week showed me right here is everything I want. But I told him earlier I wanted to get him out of my system. I said this was over when I went home. It's what I thought was right. But in the last two weeks? All that has changed.

He seems so set on the two-week timeline. Now I'm feeling he's changed his mind. And it sucks. With my brother here helping me move back and shooting the shit with Evan, it's not like I can bring it up.

I already decided I'm going to use the excuse of Kaylee needing me to get out of family dinner this weekend. It's just too fresh and I won't have my walls up enough to sit in the same room with him. Though I haven't told anyone about me missing dinner, I know Kaylee will cover for me at a moment's notice.

"Looks like this is the last bag. I swear your things multiplied while you were here," Cody says, holding my duffle bag.

"Why don't you take that to the car, and I'll do one more sweep of the house?" I'm hoping to have even just a minute alone with Evan.

"Skye, why don't you go help Uncle Cody?" Evan asks.

Fortunately, she doesn't ask questions, but runs over to Cody, takes his free hand in hers, and they head to my car.

Once they leave, I go upstairs to the room I was using with Evan close on my heels. He walks in behind me, closes the door, and then pins me to it.

The heat in his eyes has my heart racing with the hope he might say something. Maybe he will ask me to stay or at the very least say he isn't ready to end this. His eyes search mine and I try to tell him without words how I feel. That I want him and all that entails. But it's like there is a wall, and he isn't getting the message.

"One last kiss," he whispers before his lips land on mine.

I want to cry. There's no way I want this to be our last kiss. I want to yell that I changed my mind, but Cody is downstairs, and Evan seems pretty set on his choice. This is the bed I made. Now I have to sleep in it, as my mom would say.

Wrapping my arms around his neck, I put everything I have into that kiss. I don't want to leave anything on the table. When he breaks off, we are both breathing heavy. It's my last chance to say something, but I chicken out. I've always been one to let the guy take the lead, and I never chased anyone. So to be the one to make the move and say I changed my mind isn't something that comes naturally. Instead, I let the moment slip by.

"I'll go check the laundry to make sure you didn't forget anything." He opens the door and slips into the hallway.

When I check my room and the bathroom, I find a hair scrunchie and a necklace.

As stupid as it is, I leave the necklace in the bed-room. Maybe it will be a reason for him to call me. An open line of communication. If not, it's a reason to call him in a few days saying I think I left it. It's stupid and Kaylee would tell me not to, but I leave it anyway.

When I get back downstairs, I find Evan out front talking with Cody, so I join them.

"If you need anything, don't hesitate to ask," I tell Evan.

"Thank you for everything," he says, pulling me into a side hug.

"I don't want you to leave! Who will do my hair for school?" Skye says, pouting.

"Well, I taught your dad a few tricks. And when pic-ture day comes around, call me and I'll meet you at school to do something fancy," I say. Then I scoop her up into a hug.

I'm going to miss this little girl just as much as I'm going to miss Evan. She hugs me tightly, and I hug her back. Then the tears I've been holding back finally hit. Evan reaches out and wipes them from my face with a look I can't quite read on his face. When I pull away from Skye, I force a smile that I don't feel.

"Alright then, I need to head out as Kaylee is expecting me," I say, going to my car.

"Text me when you get there," Cody says, and I nod.

Growing up with protective parents and four brothers, they always want to know where I'm going and that I made it there safely. So now when I get where I'm going, it's second nature to text them. Even so, they still say it and it still makes me feel cared for every time.

The drive back to my apartment is a blur. Grabbing my tote bag, my duffle bag, along with my purse, I head upstairs, collapsing on the couch.

"Did you tell him you changed your mind?" Kaylee joins me with a margarita in each hand, giving one to me.

"No, he kept saying 'one last time'. Though there was one opening just before I left, but I chickened out." I take a huge gulp of my drink before setting it aside.

Getting drunk just doesn't hold any appeal to me tonight.

"And Cody still knows nothing?" she asks.

"Nope, and I'm glad he doesn't, since it looks like it's over. It's just better this way." I'm trying to convince myself as much as her. "Distract me?" I almost beg her.

"Well, I had my meeting with Jack this morning." She stops, pausing to take a sip of her drink.

Today she was going to come and help me, but Jack insisted on meeting this morning, so I told her to go and that I'd be fine.

"And?" I ask her and she smiles.

"He was amazing, Cal! Even though I can go back home tonight, I thought I'd stay and do a girls' night and go home tomorrow?" She says it as more of a question.

"Sounds perfect. I have no desire to be alone tonight."

"That's what I thought," Kaylee says, nodding her head, sipping more of her drink.

"Well, Jack also got the charges dropped. Apparently, Evan did a bit of digging and found out one of the rookies was working with Calvin. The rookie planted the drugs in the house, so they were there when Calvin told them to go look. Apparently, they were in a box of frozen peas."

"Evan knows you hate peas," I laugh.

"Exactly, so I knew I didn't buy any. Plus, trying to get Calvin to eat any kind of veggie, well you'd have a better chance of winning the lottery! But it really was Evan who saved my ass. The rookie is now in jail and I'm free to go."

I didn't even know Evan was working on the case. He never said a word. I assumed he wasn't talking to me about it, but also when did he have time? Every moment Skye wasn't there, we were all over each other. When Skye was home, he was focused on her. Still, he found time to get work done. Fuck! I find the perfect guy who can balance me, his kid, and work, and I just let him walk away. Of course I did. What the hell was I thinking?

"Okay, no more moping! Let's get changed into our pajamas and have some girl time. We are going to put on face masks, eat ice cream, and watch some movies until we pass out!" Kaylee giggles.

I'm happy to let Kaylee take charge of keeping my mind busy. Just like she did with my last breakup.

Only this one hurts so much worse. I feel numb to everything. But when I think of Evan, then it's a stabbing pain...right in my chest.

Chapter 26
Evan

"No, Dad, that's not it!" Skye whines.

She never whines. The last time she did it, she was sick, but she's not sick today. She is complaining for the same reason I am. I feel like shit because Calista isn't here.

She isn't here to wake up Skye, to do her hair, and bring me my coffee with a smile and a kiss. She isn't here for me to pamper and to make her breakfast.

She isn't here cheering Skye on about the outfit she's wearing. She isn't here smiling and winking at me before she walks out the door to let me know that when she gets back, we will have some fun.

She isn't here, and I'm trying and failing to do a simple braid for Skye's hair.

She isn't here. And she's missed.

"I'm sorry," I whisper, dropping her hair and meeting my daughter's eyes in the mirror.

Skye grabs the brush from the counter and brushes her hair.

"It's okay, Daddy. But maybe you should take beauty school classes because I have many more days of school before I move out." Then she runs downstairs, leaving me there looking like a fish out of water. Eyes wide, mouth opening and closing, and the reality of what she said sinks in.

I take her to school, and the entire way there, she is quiet, staring out the window. Before she jumps out of the car and practically runs into school, she gives me a forced smile.

To kill some time, I pop in at the station to say hi to Rick and Judy. Everyone is happy to see me, and the Chief even says I'm free to use the station's gym while I'm on leave and working with my physical therapist.

Then, on my way home, I stop at the bakery and stare across the street at Calista's apartment. It's dark, and I wonder if she is sleeping in. Probably, she's enjoying not having to be up at the crack of dawn to get Skye ready. She deserves to sleep in and I should be bringing her breakfast in bed.

Fuck, I miss her.

After getting my coffee, I head home. I'm not sure what to do with my days, since I'm all alone. I'm still not working, but I won't start PT until next week. When Calista was here, I'd fill my day with her. Now that she isn't at the house, I'm completely lost.

Everywhere I turn in my house, I can see her. When I try to do laundry, all I can see is Calista bent over the washing machine, switching out laundry, with her perfect ass on display.

When I try to pick up Skye's room, all I see is Calista cuddled in bed with Skye reading her books out loud before bed.

And anytime I step foot in my room, I see her flushed and gorgeous as she is coming on my cock, and I'm so hard it's uncomfortable.

All but running out of the cabin, I leave an hour early to pick Skye up from school. When I get there much earlier than I normally do, the moms there to pick up their kids gets out of their cars and come over to chat and see how I'm doing.

Normally, I'd hate it, but at least it's a distraction. Finally the kids are streaming out of the school, and I spot Skye.

She jumps into the car telling me all about her day. The books she read, her new list of spelling words, and the craft project they are working on.

"What do you want to do for dinner, Princess?"

"Pancakes!" she says.

She is much more excited than she was this morning, which is nice, but short-lived.

"What kind of pancakes? Blueberry? Apple?"

"Bananas Foster!"

My heart sinks.

Those are the ones Calista made us, and I don't have the recipe for them.

"I don't have the recipe, baby, but I'm sure we can find it online," I say. Then in my rearview mirror, I see Skye's face fall.

Once we're home, I sit at my computer, easily finding a recipe for the pancakes. I print it out and pull out what we need, setting it at the counter.

Skye joins me and makes a face. "Calista doesn't add cream to them." Skye wrinkles her nose.

Putting the cream away, I pick Skye up and set her on the counter, so we are at eye level.

"You miss her, don't you?"

I can see the sadness in her eyes.

"Yes. She fit in here, and for the first time, I got to see what it was like to have a mom." Skye's bottom lip wobbles, and I pull her in for a hug.

Maybe I was naive, thinking I was doing such a good job, and she wasn't missing out with only having a father. I hate seeing her like this, especially when I miss Calista too.

"Why don't you go work on your spelling words for a bit? We still have time before we start dinner," I say. I'm needing a few minutes to collect my thoughts.

While I know I should start dinner, I just need a breather because I can't seem to admit out loud that I miss Calista, too. And I know Skye needs to hear it.

Going upstairs, I stand in the doorway of the room that Calista stayed in. Since she left, I haven't been able to step foot in it. But I do now, and catch a whiff of her perfume.

Her stuff is gone, but it still feels like she is here. In my imagination, I can see her curled up in bed reading or smiling at me in the mirror as she puts in a pair of earrings, getting ready to take Skye to school or pick her up.

When I turn to leave, something catches my eye on the dresser behind the door. A necklace. Walking over, I pick it up and immediately know it's Calista's. I remember her wearing it.

That's when I lose it. All the emotion I was holding in bursts out of me. I'm crying in a way I haven't in years. She was never going to be temporary in my life. I knew it, and even when I had the chance to say something when she was leaving, I didn't.

"Daddy?" Skye asks, tearfully.

"I miss her too, Skye. A lot. I messed up, and I didn't ask her to stay." Unable to stand, I press my back to the wall, sliding down to the floor.

Skye comes to sit in my lap, wrapping her little arms around my neck.

"Mistakes can always be fixed, right?" she asks tentatively.

She's repeating words I've told her many times before. Only this time, I don't know if they're true.

I don't say anything because I don't know what to say.

"Do you love her, Daddy?" Skye asks, shocking the hell out of me.

I really think about it because my gut reaction is yes, I do, and that I have for longer than I want to admit. The more I think about the last few weeks, the more I realize I love that woman with every part of me, and the reason it hurts so much is that she took my heart with her when she left.

Suddenly, I see everything clearly. It's like I've been walking around in a haze of hurt that only my seven-year-old was truly able to discern.

"Yes, I do. What do you think about me marrying her?" I ask Skye.

Her face lights up with the brightest smile, one I haven't seen since Calista left.

"I was hoping you would! I love her! Are you going to ask her?" Skye says, bouncing in my lap.

At the thought of marrying Calista, I feel peace. Not the normal resistance I would feel when people would randomly ask when I was going to give Skye a mother. I love being Skye's dad and couldn't stand the thought of bringing someone in to our life and not only sharing my time with someone but also sharing Skye with someone. Now, with Calista in our lives, it feels like I'm not sharing, but widening the circle. The heartbreak I felt a moment ago is gone. It's replaced with hope that Calista feels the same way and that I will get her back soon. A plan is forming in my head and I'm not going to wait. I want my future with her to start as soon as possible.

"Will you help me pick out a ring?"

"Yes!" She jumps up.

"Okay, go put on a fancy dress and brush your hair really well."

She runs off with a happy smile on her face.

Then I head to my room, getting dressed with a satisfied smile on my face. Sending a text to Jack, I ask him to reach out to the jewelry store next door and let them know I'm coming so they don't close early. There's no way I'm leaving anything to chance.

I plan to bring Calista home. Nothing is going to stand in my way.

Chapter 27

CALISTA

After a long night of talking and drinking with Kaylee, I slept in. There was no guilt, and I enjoyed every minute of it. That is until I had to open my eyes and realize I'm at my apartment, not Evan's cabin. I've had that same feeling every minute since I left Evan's.

All I did was dream about my time with Evan, being held in his arms, and him being inside me. I woke up so damn turned on and nothing seems to fix it.

Then, the rest of the day drags on. I don't know what to do with myself. Normally, I'd be taking care of Skye and spending my day with Evan, but I have so much free time on my hands. Kaylee has to go to work, and I have nothing. I don't want to face Cody or my parents because I would have to explain why I'm so upset, and that's not a conversation I'm ready to have.

I cleaned up my apartment and unpacked, but everything I pulled out reminded me of Evan. I washed clothes, did dishes, and then sat down to try to read, thinking maybe I could get lost in someone else's problems. It worked for a while until I got hungry.

It is just after noon, so I walk down to the cafe to pick up an order and then come home to eat alone in peace. But I had to walk by the bakery where Evan and I had coffee the morning after I did Skye's hair at school.

In such a small town, it's going to be hard to not only ignore the memories of him but him as well. I'm going to have to see him at family dinners. Mom always invites him and Skye. And what about when he starts dating someone? Is he going to bring her to a family dinner? Will I be able to sit there and act like my heart isn't being ripped out?

I get my food, come home, and cry. Once I finally eat, but then I curled up back in bed, turned on the TV, and just wallowed. That is until I got a call from my brother saying he was coming by today after dinner at Mom and Dad's.

He still doesn't know about Evan and me, so it would be hard to explain me being curled up in bed all day. So, I showered and got dressed. I just finished putting on some makeup to hide the fact that I'd been crying when the doorbell rings.

I check the time and it's not even six yet. Mom nor-mally doesn't have dinner ready before six. Maybe Cody decided to stop by before dinner?

Check the peephole, I about fall over when I see Evan and Skye standing there.

I open the door and stand there stunned. Skye is dressed in a gold tulle dress with glitter flowers printed on it. She has on tights and shiny gold dress shoes. She even put on a white headband like I taught her. Evan is in a deep blue button-down shirt with the sleeves rolled up, which brings out his eyes. Why are rolled up sleeves such a damn turn on? He has on black dress pants and both are standing there with huge smiles on their faces.

"What..." I clear my throat," What are you doing here?"

My voice doesn't sound like my own as I try to hide all the emotions I'm feeling.

"Can we come in? We will explain," Evan says.

I nod and step back, holding the door open for them. They come inside and Skye runs right to the couch and bounces on it looking out the window to Main Street below.

Closing the door, I follow them into my living room. Evan walks to the middle of the room. He looks around before he turns to me with a small smile on his face. This is the first time he's been in my apartment, but I can't even find it in me to give him the grand tour because I have to know why he's here.

He walks over to me and takes my hand in his, and I tense. Skye is watching everything, and we don't so much as touch around her. But she is still looking out the window, so I try to relax.

"I went to make the banana foster pancakes you made, but the recipe I found online wasn't the right one. It caused us both to have a bit of a meltdown," Evan says.

I'm completely confused. He's smiling because he had a meltdown over a recipe? His tone is gentle and completely opposite to how I'm feeling right now.

"You could have texted me for the recipe. I'm happy to share it." I say not sure where this is going.

But he just shakes his head. "It caused Skye and me to have a talk where we made an important decision that concerns us both. And it was what I needed to get over this fear I had when you walked out the door the other day," he says.

"What did you need to talk about?" I whisper, my heart racing.

Evan looks behind him at Skye and while holding one of my hands in his, he holds his other hand out to Skye who is now watching us. She walks up and takes it.

"We realized how much we both missed you," he says.

"Daddy tried to do my hair for school, and it was really bad," Skye whispers the last part like Evan couldn't hear it standing right beside her. The love in his eyes as he looks at her really makes me melt.

"I missed you helping with Skye at bedtime, holding you in my arms, and how you just brought life to our home," Evan says.

"Well, I missed your cooking and how you did the princess voices for my books and let me wear your makeup," Skye says.

"So, Skye and I had a conversation. When I asked you to move in, it wasn't done right. But I meant it. I didn't want you to leave. So, we talked about it, and we decided we don't want you to move in," he says, and his eyes stay on mine.

I try not to let the disappointment show on my face. This whole time, the hope was building that maybe we could work things out, and in the blink of an eye, all that was crushed.

"Moving in isn't permanent enough," Evan says.

My heart takes off racing again. I don't know if I can handle much more of these up and down emotions.

Then, right there in the middle of my living room, he drops to one knee and reaches into his pocket. Skye lets out a squeal while jumping up and down and clapping her hands. My brain doesn't register what is going on as I look back at Evan.

"We talked, and we both want something much more permanent," Evan says.

"I want you to be my mom," Skye says with a huge smile.

My heart melts. I want nothing more than to be this sweet, amazing girl's mom. I see so much of myself in her, and I love her with all my heart.

"I want you to be my wife. I want to stand up in front of our friends and family and tell them how I fell in love with you years ago. When the universe pushed us together, I got a second chance to act on my feelings. I want to tell our grandkids that you saved my life, literally, and I want to give Skye a little brother or sister. I want it all with you. Will you marry me?" Evan asks.

There's no hesitation on my part because I want all of that too. I want the rest of my days spent with him, and I thought I screwed that up when I didn't say anything and walked out his door the other day.

"Yes!" I say.

Skye jumps all around my living room as Evan slides the ring on my finger.

I lean down and hug Skye first before I pull Evan into a kiss.

"Ewww! Daaad!" Skye says once she sees us.

In the back of my mind, I wonder what the people in the store downstairs are hearing, but I'm back in Evan's arms. I don't think I care much right now.

"Why don't you go try out my new lip gloss in my bathroom," I tell her, never taking my eyes off Evan's.

As Skye runs off with a delighted smile on her face. Evan kisses me again and again as if we are trying to make up for lost time.

"You know this means we have to tell my brother now, right?" I ask between kisses.

"I figured," he says, taking my hand and leading me to the couch.

He sits down and pulls me onto his lap.

"Tomorrow, I plan to go talk to him. I just want to enjoy the night with you," he says, kissing me again, this time soft and gently.

I'm so lost I don't hear my front door opening until Cody's angry voice fills the air.

"What the fuck is this?" He yells, causing me to jump up from Evan's lap.

"Cody," I say, trying to catch my breath and calm my racing heart from the almost heart attack he just gave me.

"What are you doing here?" Evan asks from behind me, his voice much calmer than I feel.

"Mom sent me with food, and I wanted to talk to her about what her plans were. I didn't realize they were swapping spit with my supposed best friend!" Cody yells.

"Keep it down. Skye is in the other room." Evan looks toward my bedroom.

"Again, I'm going to ask what the fuck is this?" Cody sets the food on the kitchen counter and motions between us.

I look at Evan, and he looks at me before wrapping an arm around my waist. We are in this together now, and this isn't the perfect moment I'm sure we both thought it would be, but it's now or never.

"I just asked her to marry me, and she said yes," Evan says.

Holding my breath, I wait to see what Cody says next.

I want him to be happy for us. To smile and pull me into a hug and officially welcome Evan to the family, even though he's basically been family this whole time.

He does none of that.

Cody stares between us, his face red and just short of steam flying from his ears. He doesn't say a word as he turns around and walks out, slamming the door behind him.

"That is not how I planned that to go," Evan says.

"You and me both," I say, staring at the door.

Chapter 28
Calista

As I stare at the door my brother slammed behind him, my mind is blank. While I should be worried that he's upset and feel bad that he found out this way, all I feel is relief that he now knows.

"In a few days, he will calm down. Tomorrow, after he's had the night to stew over it, I'll go talk to him. You know Cody holds on to his anger the longer we wait to go talk to him," Evan says.

Evan's words hardly penetrate. But I'm pulled from my fog when my phone goes off.

"I think I should go talk to Kaylee. I told her I'd come over tonight after Cody left. She still hates being alone in that house and has been scrubbing every inch of it." I tell Evan, not making eye contact.

"Okay, will you pack a bag and come stay with us tonight?" Evan asks.

"If Kaylee doesn't need me, then you won't be able to keep me away." I turn to him, giving him a pas-sionate-don't forget-me kiss.

Even though I want nothing more than to fall asleep in his arms and be there to help Skye to bed, I have a lot on my mind that I need to sort through as well.

"I'm afraid to go see what Skye has gotten into. Let's go see," Evan says.

Walking into the bathroom, we find she turned on the little radio I keep in there and has no less than ten lip glosses and lipsticks out.

"I was trying different combinations, but I think this one is my favorite," she says.

She's wearing bright pink lipstick, and over it is a little lip gloss I wear only for costumes.

"I think you look like a princess," Evan says.

I nod, trying not to smile.

"But we have to get going," Evan says.

"You're coming? Right, Calista?" Skye asks, turning to me.

"Tonight, I have to go see a friend of mine. I promised before I knew you would be here. Though if she doesn't need me, I will come your way. Otherwise, I promise to be there at school to do your hair in the morning. No matter what," I wink at her.

That seems to be all she needs because she takes his hand and pulls him toward the door.

"Okay, Daddy, let's go!"

"Be safe and let me know when you get there and what your plans are, so I'm not up all night worrying about you, okay?" Evan says, giving me one last kiss for the road.

Watching them go, I head to my room and pack a bag because I have every intention of being at their house tonight. I don't want to come back to my place if I don't have to.

Once I get my stuff loaded in the car, I head toward Kaylee's.

As I pass the road that leads to Cody's place, I make a quick decision. Instead of going to Kaylee's, I'm going to Cody's. Right now, when I'm angry is the perfect time to confront Cody.

When I pull into Cody's driveway, his truck is there. Going up to his door, I knock loudly and repeatedly until he answers the door.

"The fuck Cal! What is it?"

I push my way in.

"I'm not going to be moving in with Mom and Dad. I'm moving in with Evan and, for the first time in my life, doing what I want. While I cared for Grandma and Grandpa on my own, our family took a step back and let me do it. Do you know what that was like?" I ask.

"Calista..." he starts, but I cut him off.

"It was like being given two large kids and having no help. If I wanted to so much as go to the grocery store, I had to find someone to sit with them. I had no social life and no friends. If I had even had a chance to meet a guy, there was no way to have him over to the house or develop any sort of relationship. I. Had. No. Life.

Then I looked up and I'm in my thirties. I was back in my hometown, with no relationship, husband, or kids. All of which I wanted before I turned thirty. And now you guys want me to move in and take care of more people, and you have the nerve to be mad that I finally did something for myself?"

"I didn't...."

"No, what you didn't do was think about me. You didn't want to give up your social life, so you expected me to give up mine. But here is a news flash. I'm not going to give up my life anymore. Right now, Mom and Dad don't need help, but when they do, it won't be me moving in. So when that day arrives, you and the guys better step up because it's your turn." I cross my arms and finally pause, giving him a chance to talk.

"I didn't know you couldn't have a social life." He looks rueful as he sits on the couch.

"Because you never came to visit. I was promised you guys would come to help, but no one ever did. Though Mom and Dad did visit once a year. Some social life. You weren't willing to give up your twenties to take care of someone," I say.

I know Cody was out sleeping around and having a good time at parties, rodeos, and who knows what else.

"I'm sorry. Of course, we will help when the time comes," he says.

"No, you will take care of it, and I will be the one helping. But it's my turn to be selfish. I plan to have a family while I still can. That will take priority. Now, as far as Evan. Yes, we should have told you, but we didn't because we knew this would be your reaction, and we didn't know if it would work out. Plus, how DARE you tell anyone I'm off-limits? It's for me to decide. If you hadn't been a jerk about that, we could have both been happier sooner!" I say heatedly.

I know it's not fair to put that all on him, but I'm fuming, and I want to get my point across.

"Evan, really?" Cody snorts. "I asked you to help him. My best friend!"

"So, we should remain unhappy just so you can be happy? If that is how you want to keep thinking, you are about to lose a lot more than just the two of us," I say, standing prepared to walk out the door.

"Wait. How..." I turn to look at Cody, and he's sitting on the edge of his seat and looking down at his feet with his arms resting on his legs. I wait for him to ask his question.

"How did it happen?" he asks.

"When I came home the first night, he was the cop who arrived at the accident scene where that lady crashed. We talked some, but that was it.

Then, when he was lying on the ground bleeding out, something shifted. Even though I had people I knew come into the ER before, I was able to focus and do what needed done. But it was different this time," I say.

"Even so, neither of us acted on it. But being in close proximity was difficult. One night when I was changing his bandage, it all came to a head. Damn, it was just a kiss. But you know what the first thing we both thought of? Yeah, it was you. The first kiss I've had in years, and I had to feel guilty about it because of you!" I sit on the chair beside the couch because I'm not sure my legs will hold me, I'm so angry.

"Then Skye had a sleepover and that's when we decided to give in and get it out of our system. When I moved out, it ended. Only by then, we had both fallen in love. Evan showed up tonight to propose and that was the first time I'd seen him since I left."

"And Skye?" He asks, the anger from his voice gone.

"I love that girl as if she was my own. She didn't know what was going on. We kept it from her. But she's important in this new life we want. So part of the proposal was to ask me to be her mom," I say.

Cody sits there without speaking, but the silence is uncomfortable.

"And if this doesn't work out?" he finally asks. "Does he lose his entire support group?" Cody looks grim.

"These are questions that I went over and over in my head. He only loses them if you let him, but Cody, this is happening. It's not just dating. We are getting married. The question is, are you going to be supportive and part of our lives, or are you going to let your anger ruin it all?"

Cody bounces his feet while still staring at the ground.

I can tell he's trying to process, and maybe I should have let it be until tomorrow like Evan said. But that would mean I wouldn't have been able to sleep, and I'm not going to sit on this to make Cody feel better.

"Listen, I'm not happy about how I found out or about this in general, but I want you both happy. If that means together, then just know it better work out. There is no option for it not to be a forever thing," Cody says, smirking.

"There is the self-centered brother I love," I say sarcastically.

Giving him a hug, I walk to my car. Once in, I call Kaylee.

"Hey girl, are you on your way?" "How mad would you be if I ditched you tonight?" I'm parked at the end of Cody's road, waiting for her answer.

"Depends on the reason?" she says.

Since I know she will forgive me for this one, I point my car away from Kaylee's toward Evan's cabin.

"Well, Evan showed up with Skye, he proposed, and then Cody walked in. Predictably, he went off about finding out and the whole best friend thing. He stormed out, and I couldn't go through the night without confronting him. So, after putting him in his place, we talked it out," I say.

Then I hear a thump on her end of the line, but otherwise the line is quiet.

"You still there?" I ask.

"You have to tell a girl to sit down before dumping all that on her. Holy Shit! Holy. Shit." she exclaims.

"Yes, I had to take a minute to process what you just told me. Okay, so start at the beginning, and don't leave out any details."

I tell her everything and finish just before I get to Evan's.

"Wow. So, you're going to Evan's tonight, right?" she asks.

"Of course," I say.

"Good. As your promised maid of honor, decided when we were sixteen, I will start pulling location ideas for the wedding. When I see you in a few days, I will have found some wedding dress shops in Helena and will have a bunch of stuff ready for you to look at."

Laughing, I say, "But just to make it official, Kaylee will you do me the honor of being my maid of honor? I can't do this without you."

"Yes!" She says, giggling.

"Okay. I'm at Evans, so I will talk to you tomorrow."

"I'm so happy for you!" she says, hanging up.

Before I even get the car turned off, Evan is at the front door. I'm smiling big at him as he walks toward me.

"I thought you were going to text me to let me know you made it okay and what your plans are," Evan says.

He doesn't sound very happy. But shit, I did forget to text him. I was too fueled by sibling anger.

"Yes, but..." I start.

Surprising me, he picks me up and tosses me over his good shoulder.

"No buts. I don't like worrying about you and now you will deal with your punishment," Evan says carrying me upstairs to his room.

Now our room.

I have the biggest smile on my face because punish-ment or not, this is the life I've been waiting for, and I plan to enjoy every moment.

Chapter 29
EVAN

I loved waking up and having Calista in my arms. No more hiding from anyone. It felt so free. Skye seemed to accept it with no problems.

Though she had some questions this morning like can she still come in if she has a bad dream. Yes, we told her. Can she still come in my bedroom? Yes, but she has to knock first. Can she still use my bathtub? Yes. Can she still use Calista's hair stuff and makeup? We agreed with a yes. Though I wasn't thrilled with the makeup.

It was so much easier to say no when I only had one person giving me puppy dog eyes. Now that the two of them can gang up against me, I'm hopeless. I have to give in. And I wouldn't have it any other way.

After we got Skye off to school today, Calista said she was going to go check on Kaylee. So I decided now was the time to talk to Cody. I don't want this hanging over our heads any longer than it has to be, and there isn't anything I wouldn't do for my girls.

That thought makes me smile. My girls. The two people in the whole world who own a part of my heart. I think Calista owned that part of my heart a lot longer than either of us realized. Being able to admit it to her now is the most freeing feeling.

Stopping at Cody's house first, I hope to catch him before he heads to the distillery for the day. Less people to witness if he attacks me because I completely deserve it.

Thankfully, his truck is in the driveway, so I knock. He opens the door and frowns at me. He looks like he hasn't slept. His hair is messy and there are dark circles under his eyes.

"Can I come in? I think we need to talk," I say.

Cody doesn't say anything, just stands to the side and holds the door open for me. Once inside, I go right to the living room before sitting on the couch.

"If you weren't injured, I'd punch you right now," Cody says, standing in the doorway.

"And I'd have let you. This isn't a fling. I've liked her since we were in high school. But with the age gap and you, I never said anything. Yet seeing her again after all this time? It was brutal." I take a quick glance at Cody and he seems to be listening.

As I keep talking, he moves to sit in the recliner facing me.

"Nothing happened prior to her staying with me. We talked, she did Skye's hair, but that was it. Once she moved in, it kept building. We both fought it long and hard, which isn't easy when you are in such close quarters. Until we gave in and kissed. That first kiss? It rocked our worlds. After that, I think I knew then it would be a forever kind of thing.

Even though we planned to end it when she left, I couldn't. So last night, Skye and I went and asked her to marry me. She said yes and then you walked in." I lay everything on the table.

He doesn't say anything, so I go on.

"Skye loves her, and I don't think I realized until Calista was staying with us how much Skye has wanted a mother figure. When I asked how she felt about me marrying Calista, you should have seen the smile on her face. I haven't seen one so big from her since we took her to Branson," I tell him.

Cody looks up, studying me. Even though it makes me feel uncomfortable, as a cop I know I need to ride the silence out. Before I let him speak, there is one more thing I want to say.

"I love her. And I plan to marry her. Having you on our side would make things easier. But don't ask me to choose because I won't."

Having said what I wanted to, I'm perfectly content to sit in the silence and wait for him to speak.

"Well, at least your story matches hers," he says.

I sit here shocked. "What do you mean?"

"She came over her last night madder than a wasp in a coke can. Then she proceeded to lay into me and tell me what happened. I've been up all-night thinking about it," Cody says.

I'm stunned. She didn't tell me she came here.

Picking up my phone, I shoot her a text.

> Me: Why didn't you tell me you went and talked to Cody last night?

Thankfully, her answer is quick.

> Calista: You didn't let me get a word out before we went upstairs…

Well shit, if it isn't true. Maybe I should have let her speak before I let my anger and worry take over. But what a damn good night it was.

"Listen, I want you both happy," Cody says. "But that doesn't mean I'm happy about all this. And for a while, I reserve the right to be pissed at how I found out. Let me make some things very clear. I'm on her side. Despite what I might tell her. You hurt her and I will murder you and smile in my mug shot," he says, glaring at me.

"I don't doubt it," I say.

"When you are healed, I still reserve the right to punch you," he adds.

"We can sell tickets and make it an event," I say, smirking. I'm okay with our conversation. I've said my piece and Cody knows where I stand.

"Well, you have always been family. I guess we might as well make it official. Besides, I can't have Calista mad at me for this for too long..." he says, a slight blush on his face.

"What am I missing?" I ask.

"There might be someone, but she's connected to Cal. With how things went over and how I reacted, I'm not at all sure how my news will go over. I guess we'll just have to see," he sighs.

"Well, whatever you do, don't tell me what you don't want her to know. I'm pretty sure I signed an oath in blood to tell her everything from now on. If I had to choose, I'd rather have you mad at me than her. For reasons we won't talk about, since she is your sister."

Cody tosses a throw pillow at me, but has a smile on his face.

"Well, I'm not ready to talk about it anyway," Cody says.

"So, are we good?" I ask hesitantly.

Cody nods, "Yeah, we are good. But there was something else I wanted to talk to you about."

"What's that?"

"Listen, I've talked with my brothers and Dad about this. But, not Cal, so that is a talk for you two. Since you will be family soon, this is even better timing," he says.

"I don't know if I'm interested or scared..." I say, several things racing through my head.

"When you told me you didn't want Skye to worry about you, I heard your concern. And selfishly, I don't want to worry about you either. Definitely, I know Cal won't want to either. I know my sister. After seeing you having been shot, she won't do well with you going back to work. If it's what you want, she will hide it. But know, she will be a wreck," Cody says.

My mind starts racing and whirling with what that means. I was worried enough about going back to work when it was just Skye. Now, I have to consider Calista too. Skye only has hospital images in her head, but Calista saw the worst of it. I can't do that to her...

"Evan!" Cody yells my name, jerking me from my careening thoughts.

"Fuck," I say, trying to take deep breaths. I realize I was on the edge of a full-blown panic attack. It's been years since I had one, but I know what they feel like.

"You okay?" Cody asks.

"I will be. Sorry about that." I try to get us back on track and my mind focused on something else.

"Where did your mind go just then?"

"To the fact that it's not just Skye and me I have to worry about anymore. Calista was there and saw all of it. I can't do that to her again." My voice is hoarse as I imagine a similar scenario.

"Well then, I might have a solution. After the BBQ competition, the distillery business increased more than we planned. We need help full-   time. We'd like to keep the ranks close, and would like for you to join us," Cody says.

"Doing what?" He has my interest, but I don't know what he has in mind.

"A manager role. Preferably mornings. We need to open earlier and get the employees in to make more products. But you know none of us are morning people. Colt has already said he's happy to stay later. He overshared telling me that it's a good way to pick up woman to take home. I thought since you are up early with Skye taking her to school, you might be interested. We'll need you for mornings. Monday through Friday and afternoon hours are flexible. Mom is happy to keep picking up Skye, but if you need to run out, I'm in by eleven most days.

We have an idea of what you earn at the station, and we can offer you more. However, I'm not sure we can match the benefits. If you are interested, talk it over with Cal. We'd like to bring her in to do front of the house stuff. Growing up, she loved decorating, so it will suit her. She'll be doing other tasks as well, but you won't be her direct boss. Though she might have her own plans. We can talk more later," Cody says.

My head is spinning. Before Calista, I'd have accepted on the spot. But he's right. I need to talk to her.

"While I know I'll have to talk to Calista, I am very interested," I say.

We've said everything we're going to say, so we stand and give each other a half hug, saying good-bye.

When I get to my car, I check my phone. Calista said she was going home about ten minutes ago, so she should get there before me. It's not even lunchtime, so we have plenty of time before Skye gets out of school.

> Me: I'm heading home now. I expect to find you naked in our bed, waiting. After I give us both the relief I know we need, I have a lot to talk to you about.

I'm halfway home when she replies with a photo of her clothes on the ground in a pile beside the bed. This woman is going to keep me on my toes.

Chapter 30

Calista

It's been a few days since Evan talked to Cody and we are going to family dinner. Tonight, we plan to come clean to my parents and my brothers about us.

Evan and I have also talked in detail about Cody's offer for Evan to work at the distillery. It's a lot to think about and consider. He told me how he's been feeling about having to go back to work and his thoughts on what Skye and I would go through. I assured him if it's what he wanted, we could handle it and I'd be there for her.

After much discussion and talking, we both finally feel at peace with the choice we made. Tonight we plan to talk to Cody about it, too.

"Wear one of your flowy skirts and comfortable shoes," Evan says as I'm getting ready. He winks at me and then leaves telling me he has something planned.

I do as he asks and then help Skye do her hair. She is sitting on the bathroom counter facing the mirror with a big grin on her face, giggling as she tells me about some girl name Violet in her class. When I look up, I see Evan leaning against the bathroom door frame with a smile on his lips. When he catches me watching him, he walks up behind me and wraps his arms around my waist and rests his chin on my shoulder.

"Don't move," I tell them and reach for my phone, snapping our first official family photo. It may be in a mirror and in the bathroom, but it's of us and that's what matters.

"We should book a family photo shoot. You guys can wear long flowy dresses and even dress me up," he says, kissing my cheek.

"Yes!" Skye's clearly on board.

"I might know someone for that," I wink at him.

Then we walk to the car and head to my parents house. It's warm and we don't need jackets, but I grab them anyway because the temperature drops fast once the sun goes down.

On the way to my parents house, Skye sings along to the radio, and Evan and I are content to let her. It's comfortable being with Evan, holding hands and enjoying Skye entertaining us. Every so often I look over at him and I can't believe he's mine. I know there might be some resistance today about our news, but we will face it together.

We are the last to arrive, and Skye immediately runs off, soaking up everyone's attention. We get a few looks about arriving together, but no one says anything.

"Okay! It's dinner time and you can all chat and gossip at the table!" Mom calls after she says hi to Skye.

Cody and I swap seats so I can sit next to Evan. This time Dad doesn't let it go.

"Why are we playing musical chairs?" Dad asks.

"Because apparently those two are getting married," Cody says, smirking.

I have to admit that I'm surprised when the whole table erupts with cheers and talking until a piercing whistle fills the air.

I know that whistle. It's Dad, and he's used it a few times over the years to get our attention.

"I didn't think you'd ask her so soon, but I'm glad you did," Dad says, and my jaw drops.

"You don't think I'd have asked you to marry me without talking to your dad first, did you?" Evan asks.

"Was that the day you sent Skye out of the room with me? When was she wearing her gold dress?" Mom asks.

"Yep. I went and proposed right then and there," Evan reaches for my hand at the table.

Mom wants to see my ring, so I show it off, proving I said yes.

"I didn't even know you two were dating." Colt says from my other side, giving me a side hug.

"Neither did I," Cody says, still smiling.

My brothers freeze.

"How is he still standing?" Drew asks.

"Oh, he has it coming once he's not a cripple anymore. But we eventually worked it out," Cody says.

"Yeah, once she said yes, I went to talk with him. Though maybe I should have had it with him sooner," Evan says.

"I had no idea you two were dating! Tell me everything," Mom demands, as she passes the food around.

The next few minutes I tell her how it all happened. Though I make sure to keep it PG and use a few code words for the little ears in the room.

"It's so romantic!" Mom says with a sigh.

"Also, if you are absolutely sure you want me working at the distillery, I'd like to take you up on it," Evan says to Cody.

The table goes quiet, with everyone looking at Cody.

"Hell, yeah! You are the only one we trust in that role besides Calista. But we all know she doesn't want that job," Cody says.

I wrinkle my nose at him. I'd do it to help him out, but it really isn't my thing.

"Cal, if you don't have any other commitments, we would love to have you help out with decorating, designing the new add on, and working the retail store and inventory. Completely flexible hours and four brothers on call to move anything you need," Cody says. Then he teasingly flutters his eyes at me.

"How can I say no to that? Something flexible sounds great especially around wedding planning and getting settled." I look at Evan to see his reaction.

"It's perfect," he says, kissing me on the cheek.

"They do that a lot," Skye says to my mom, making everyone at the table laugh.

"Well, now that Evan has gone after what he wants, it's time for you to do the same Cody." Dad gives him a pointed look.

They stare at each other for a moment before Cody nods. Then, as quickly as it came up, the subject is dropped.

"Any idea what that's about?" I whisper to Evan.

"Nope, but he's hinted at a possible girl. No idea who," Evan whispers back.

Interesting. I know Cody though. He won't share a thing until he's ready.

The rest of dinner is filled with distillery talk and some wedding discussion thrown in.

Once dinner is finished, Evan pulls me aside.

"Let's sneak out. Cody said he'd cover for us," Evan says trying to pull me to the back door.

"Where are we going?" I stop until he answers me.

"To the one place I ever saw you truly free growing up," he says.

Instantly, I know what he's talking about.

"Take Me to the Valley, Fiancé," I say, and he smiles.

We decide to walk because the weather is so nice. It's a short hike through the trees from my parents' backyard. But growing up I'd spend hours here reading on a blanket in the sun or dancing with my Walkman among the wildflowers.

And Evan is right. It's the one place I truly felt free. He caught me out here a few times when I'd sneak off, but he never told anyone that this is where I'd sneak off to. Though I suspect my parents knew.

We stop as we near the edge of the trees and the valley appears with the first batch of wildflowers of the season.

"I think this is where we should get married," Evan says as we stop and stare at the field. He walks up behind me, wrapping his arms around me and setting his chin on my shoulder. I'm finding he is doing this frequently, and I really like it.

"This is where I fell for you. Watching you here was something I couldn't get enough of, and made my crush grow," he says.

"I remember finding you out here," I smile.

"There were many times you never saw me. I liked to hide behind this tree here," he says. Turning, he pushes my back up against one of the large trees in the area.

He kisses me with such desire and love that my heart feels like it's going to explode with happiness. This is a full circle moment. Back then, those kids had no idea what was coming.

"I think this is the perfect spot to get married," I say, smiling up at him.

"Then I think we need to consummate it just to be sure." Evan says it with a wicked smile and his eyes burning hot.

"Evan, anyone could come out here!"

Ignoring me, he moves to the side of the tree to hide us from the path.

"They won't." He pulls my shirt and bra off along with his shirt. "We just need to be quick."

This man is going to be the death of me in the best possible way.

In a split second, he's pulling my skirt and panties off as he falls to his knees in front of me. Then his head is between my thighs. Fuck, the things this man can do with his mouth. Before I can catch my breath, he has me coming all over his tongue.

Then both our phones are going off, breaking the silence. Enjoying my post orgasm buzz, I let him check his phone.

"Time to go back," he says.

I reach for him. I want to take care of him before we go, but he grabs my wrist gently.

"Not right now. Trust me, when we get home and get Skye to bed, you won't be getting much sleep," he smirks.

We get dressed quickly and hike back to my parents' house. Only slightly disheveled.

Yeah, for the foreseeable future, I think we'll be getting less sleep because we can't keep our hands off each other. I was beginning to think I'd waited too long and missed my chance.

But who knew it started in this valley all those years ago, and I just had to look up and see it.

Epilogue

CALISTA

It's been a few weeks since we told my family about us and I'm at my apartment today packing up. Slowly, I've been moving stuff to Evan's. Usually, I drop Skye off at school each morning and come over. But today is Saturday, and I had breakfast at the cafe with Kaylee. So, I figured I'd grab a few things before going back to get ready for the barbeque we are having for all the mountain men and their families.

Most of them know we are engaged, but we want to make sure to tell them and invite them to the wedding.

Kaylee was so excited when I told her where we were wanting to get married. My mom cried when she heard our story and said it was perfect. Kaylee is a hopeless romantic, so she was on board. I think she   and my mom are working together now to make it happen. I'm happy to give her the reins because there is so much to do. Cake, flowers, food, decorations, rentals, invitations, save the dates, music, and the list goes on and on. Kaylee helped her cousin plan her wedding last year, so she knows exactly what to do and I will take full advantage of that knowledge.

I'm going over everything Kaylee and I talked about this morning, and I'm so lost in my head I almost miss the knocking on my door. I open it to find Cole, Axel, Emelie, Hope, and Cash there.

"Evan sent us to help with the packing and to bring all your stuff to the cabin," Emelie says bouncing in to give me a hug.

"I think he doesn't like you having your place still. It's making him feel unsettled, so he enlisted our help," my brother says.

"Most of the furniture stays. Though I'm shocked at how many possessions I've accumulated since I moved here." I start directing them to what stays and what goes.

About an hour later, everything is packed and in my car and the guys' trucks. Kaylee said she'd help me clean it on Monday and then I can turn my keys in.

When we get to the cabin, Jana, Phoenix, Jenna, and Jack and Sage are already there. When they see us, they come out to help with the boxes as Evan walks over to me.

"Thank you for arranging the help," I say, kissing him.

"I just want you here and settled as soon as possible and the guys were happy to help."

Bennett, Willow, Storm, and River show up just as we get the last of the boxes into the house. We all gather in the backyard where there is seating and the grill. I've never seen so many people here at once, but it feels right.

Skye is in seventh heaven with the other children around. She's taken to Emelie and likes to be with her. Right now, Skye's playing with their son, Noah, who isn't quite a year old yet. Skye can get that boy to laugh like no one else. Someday, she's going to be a great big sister.

"Go mingle. We can unpack later," Evan says kissing me on the cheek before heading off toward the grill.

"Hey, we were just talking about our summer trip to the lake," Emelie says patting the spot on the wicker sofa next to her.

"What?" I ask, sitting down.

"It's a tradition we started where we all spend a few days at the lake at the back of Cash and Hope's property. We camp, swim, and we read in the sun, while the men hunt. It's a great way to relax in the middle of the summer chaos of winter prep. You guys will be joining us, right?" Willow asks.

"Oh Um... I..." I glance over at Evan. I don't want to commit to something he hadn't planned.

Evan's eyes meet mine and it's like he can read my mind.

Walking over to us, he asks, "What's up?" His eyes are focused on mine.

"They were talking about their trip to the lake and asked if we were going," I say.

"I already cleared it with Cody so long as you want to go," he says.

I smile and turn back to the girls.

"It sounds like fun," I say.

"Yes!" Skye claps, and everyone giggles.

"Skye, do you know how to swim?" Jenna asks.

"Yep, Daddy and Nana taught me before I even started school," she says with a proud smile.

"Well, what about making quilts? Any interest? We normally make a few baby quilts while we are there," Willow says.

"I've never made a quilt. Will you teach me?" Skye asks eagerly.

"And me?" I'm thinking this might be something Skye and I can learn together.

"I'd love to teach you! They sell well at Jack's shop. Even with all of us doing them, he can't keep them in stock. The tourists love handmade quilts from 'The Women of The Mountains.' That's how Sage pushes them in the store," Willow says, nodding toward Sage, Jacks wife.

We talk and chat for hours. The kids all end up inside either asleep or barely holding their eyes open watching TV in the living room.

"We don't want to be nosey, but we were wondering about Skye's birth mother." Emelie says gently.

"I don't know much about her other than she left them to go be some big Hollywood actress. Though she hasn't really made it. Evan reached out to her just last week about signing off on me adopting Skye outright. She didn't want to talk to Skye or me, but agreed to sign the papers after we were married. I was surprised when she said she was glad Skye would have a mother figure and was sorry it couldn't be her."

"Wow." The women sit there speechless.

"My mom said some people just aren't wired to have kids because they can't focus on anyone outside of themselves," I say. "It sounds like Skye's mother did the best thing she could and left. If she had tried to force herself, it would have been much more traumatic."

"That's true. My mom was like that. Granted my dad left too, but I think my grandma would have taken me and my life would have been much different. I wouldn't have been kidnapped by her for sure," Hope says.

"But then you may never have ended up here with us either." Jana wraps an arm around her.

"Well, I'd like to think I would have because this is where I was meant to be. But it just might have happened differently," Hope smiles.

"You two started working at the distillery, right?" River asks.

"Yeah, Evan is loving it so far, and has lots to learn. But I will say Skye and I breathe easier when he walks out the door now."

"How did the station take it?" Jenna asks.

"He was at his ten-year mark, and since he was injured, and the Chief is a family friend, he did a little magic on the paperwork and got him medically retired. But really, his arm probably will never get back to the regulated ninety percent to go back to active duty. So he will be able to collect a partial retirement when he hits a certain age."

"What is the prognosis on his arm?" Emelie asks.

"He's still working with the physical therapist, and she recommended a friend of hers in Helena. They're thinking that maybe going once a month for a few specialized treatments might help his arm. The hope is that his arm function will get very close to ninety-five percent, if not more."

"Wait, I'm confused," Hope says.

"Okay," I say. "With his PT here in town saying she couldn't get him over ninety percent, it made him eligible to be medically retired. Once that happened, she referred him to the one in Helena and we got the better predicted recovery. But it's speculation, remember." I say.

"Hah." The women all smiled.

"How do you like the distillery?" River asks, changing the subject.

"You could tell it was owned by men. They didn't take advantage of the small details. So, I'm working on redecorating pretty much every space and we are already planning our Christmas retail. Much of it can be done at home, which I love. If I need something, I'll text Evan to send me a picture of this or that. It saves me   from having to go in," I giggle.

"Well, I don't drink Whiskey, but if you can encourage them to get some more flattering women's clothes, I'd be happy to wear them and promo them any day," Sage says.

The other girls nod their heads in agreement.

"We are on the same wavelength! I have a few women's hoodie samples coming. You'll have to come by when they get here and give me your thoughts," I say.

We talk well into the night. To cap off a wonderful evening, we get the first peek of the neon colored sunsets that summer brings in Montana.

It's a perfect night and the perfect way to start off my perfect forever.

Get a bonus scene of Evan and Calista that features an update on all the mountain men of Whiskey River by **joining my newsletter!**

https://www.kacirose.com/Valley-Bonus-Scene

Thank you for reading the Mountain Men of Whiskey River! Get Cody's story in the spin off series, Whiskey Secrets, starting with the book **Whiskey Whispers!**

Start reading from the Mountain Men of Whiskey River from the beginning with **Take Me To The River**.

If you are up for another injured hero you will love **Saving Noah,** a scarred military hero.

Other Books by Kaci Rose

See all of Kaci Rose's Books

Mountain Men of Whiskey River

Take Me To The River – Axel and Emelie

Take Me To The Cabin – Phoenix and Jenna

Take Me To The Lake – Cash and Hope

Taken by The Mountain Man - Cole and Jana

Take Me To The Mountain – Bennett and Willow

Take Me To The Cliff – Jack and Sage

Take Me To The Edge – Storm and River

Take Me To The Valley – Evan and Calista

Oakside Military Heroes Series

Saving Noah – Lexi and Noah

Saving Easton – Easton and Paisley

Saving Teddy – Teddy and Mia

Saving Levi – Levi and Mandy

Saving Gavin – Gavin and Lauren

Saving Logan – Logan and Faith

Saving Zane – Zane and Carlee

Oakside Shorts

Saving Mason - Mason and Paige

Saving Ethan – Bri and Ethan

Saving Luke – Luke and Brooke
Saving Jake – Jake and Kassi
Saving Caden – Caden and Lucy

Club Red – Short Stories

Daddy's Dare – Knox and Summer

Sold to my Ex's Dad - Evan and Jana

Jingling His Bells – Zion and Emma

Watching You – Ella, Brooks, Connor, and Finn

Club Red: Chicago

Elusive Dom - Carter and Gemma

Forbidden Dom – Gage and Sky

Mountain Men of Mustang Mountain
(Series Written with Dylann Crush and Eve London)
February is for Ford – Ford and Luna
April is For Asher – Asher and Jenna
June is for Jensen – Jensen and Courtney
August is for Ace – Ace and Everly
October is for Owen – Owen and Kennedy
December is for Dean – Dean and Holly

Mustang Mountain Riders
(Series Written with Eve London)
February's Ride With Bear – Bear and Emerson
April's Ride With Stone – Stone and Addy

June's Ride With Lightning – Lightnight and Piper
August's Ride With Arrow – Arrow and Kathrine
October's Ride With Atlas
December's Ride With ScardaB

Bad Boys of Mustang Mountain
(Series Written with Eve London)
January's Bad Boy – Shane and Caitlin
March's Bad Boy – TY
May's Bad Boy – Kody
July's Bad Boy – Blaze
September's Bad Boy – Cooper
November's Bad Boy – Kacen

Chasing the Sun Duet

Sunrise – Kade and Lin

Sunset – Jasper and Brynn

Midnight – Nate

Rock Stars of Nashville

She's Still The One – Dallas and Austin

Accidental Series

Accidental Sugar Daddy – Owen and Ellie

The Billionaire's Accidental Nanny - Mari and Dalton

The Italian Mafia Princesses

Midnight Rose - Ruby and Orlando

Blood Red Rose – Aria and Matteo

Standalone Books

Texting Titan - Denver and Avery

Stay With Me Now – David and Ivy

Committed Cowboy – Whiskey Run Cowboys

Stalking His Obsession - Dakota and Grant

Falling in Love on Route 66 - Weston and Rory

Stalked By The Rebel – Chance and Jessa

Connect with Kaci Rose

Website

Kaci Rose's Book Shop

Join Kaci's Influencer Team

Facebook

Kaci Rose Reader's Facebook Group

TikTok

Instagram

Goodreads

Book Bub

Join Kaci Rose's VIP List (Newsletter)

About Kaci Rose

Kaci Rose writes steamy contemporary romances mostly set in small towns. She grew up in Florida but now lives in a cabin in the mountains of East Tennessee.

She is a mom to five kids, a rescue dog who is scared of his own shadow, a sleepy old hound who adopted her, and a reluctant indoor cat. Kaci loves to travel, and her goal is to visit all 50 states before she turns 50. She has 17 more to go, mostly in the Midwest and on the West Coast!

She also writes steamy cowboy romances as Kaci M. Rose.

Please Leave a Review!

I love to hear from my readers! Please **head over to your favorite store and leave a review** of what you thought of this book! Reviews are also appreciated on BookBub and Goodreads!

Made in the USA
Columbia, SC
09 February 2025

52986465R00174